Strings Attached

NOEL BAILEY

Edited by Milly Bellegris

Proofread by Megan Cox

Cover design by Bring Design

www.authornoelbailey.com

For Milly—my fearless developmental editor, who has walked beside me through dozens of books and even a genre shift. Thank you for always championing my stories and seeing their potential, even when they're still in their awkward teenage phase, waiting to grow into their true selves.

And for being the first to say: Dean deserves a book of his own.

This one's for you.

Author's Note

Welcome back to Magnolia Cove!

This book has a little bit of everything I love—slow-burn chemistry, music laced with magic, and a grumpy hero whose heart is softer than he'll ever admit. And it carries the quiet wonder of my favorite season, when the air smells of cinnamon and the world glows with gold.

But it also explores deeper notes: burnout, family ties, and what it means to risk love when you've sworn to keep your heart safe.

You'll find cozy dinners, sharp banter, a few mild curse words, and familiar Magnolia Cove faces (yes, Alex is still protective and Ethan is still baking). There are also some tender romantic moments—more swoony than steamy—that I hope make you smile.

At its heart, this book is about trust—the kind that asks you to let go of fear, lean into connection, and believe that some melodies are worth the risk.

I hope these pages wrap you in warmth and leave you carrying a little more magic when you reach the end.

With love and a playlist of stormy sonatas and stolen duets,

-Noel

Music Playlist

A playlist that hums with stormy cello notes and whispers of magic, glows with the golden light of autumn, and swells with the ache of trust slowly taking root. These songs are the perfect soundtrack to Missy and Dean's story.

Click here to listen now!

Missy

All I want is to feel a little magic for once in my life.

The thought surprises the breath from me as I lift my cello and move across the stage. Applause still echoes from the crowd from the previous piece. Beside me, Jules walks with a wild grin, his violin already lifted to his shoulder.

He lives for this moment—the technically challenging finale, the flood of lights cascading from above, sweat trailing down our spines, and thousands of eyes fixed on us like a collective spotlight.

Jules glances my way. Waiting for me to begin. He cocks a golden eyebrow, offering a steadying grin. I nod, draw in a breath, and sink into the chair, bow poised across the strings.

I've practiced Kodály's Duo for Violin and Cello until I've perfected it. The audience disappears and the golden hues of the iconic Berlin Philharmonic fade. All that's left is the music. My body moving in time with it. My arms and shoulders diving into the song.

When it's over, the audience explodes with applause. I stand to my feet, ensconced by the roaring ovation. Jules walks over to me and throws an arm around my shoulder. It's a casual enough interaction that we've had people speculate if we're dating.

We're not.

Though not because Jules would object.

Camera shutters click as the applause seems to go on for lifetimes. This is my moment—the one I've fought for my entire life. I'm the principal cellist on a prestigious tour on her final night playing in an iconic performance hall I'd only ever dreamed of visiting.

And I'm completely and utterly miserable.

Because this was supposed to be it. The dream. The moment everything would click into place and I'd finally feel whole, fulfilled, *enough*. But instead, I feel stretched thin. Like I've been running on empty through cities that blur together, chased by deadlines, praise, and a spotlight that's too hot and too bright. The music still matters—but somewhere along the way, I lost the part of myself that used to come alive when I played.

Finally, we exit the stage. As soon as the soundproof door closes, blissful quiet surrounds. A heater hums and stage crew speak in low muffled voices in the distance.

My cello tugs at my shoulder, a weight that has grown into a stone as the performance adrenaline washes from my body. I need to find a drink of water and get out of these clothes.

"Darling, that was your best performance yet." Jules slings his violin case across his shoulder and swipes his bangs from his forehead. He ends every performance looking like an Olympian, while sweat-dampened hair plasters to my forehead and I'm red-cheeked and breathless.

"You performed beautifully as always." I assume he did, anyway. I have a bad habit of dissociating while on stage. Something about the pressure to be perfect, to never miss a note, turns performance into survival. There's no one that worries over Jules' performance like Jules, though. Considering his cocky grin has remained firmly in place, I'm certain his assessment is true.

"Sinclair, Bouchard." Our stage manager calls from down the hall, headset still in place. "You two were on fire!"

"Thanks, David," Jules answers for both of us. While I'm a wilted flower after performances, Jules is ready to hit the town. But I'm wrecked. Every show feels like I'm holding my breath for ninety minutes straight—trying not to falter, not to disappoint, not to let the critics find a single crack. By the time we take our bows, all I want is silence. To disappear into my dressing room, peel off the costume of confidence, and collapse into sleep that never quite feels restful.

"Ah, the final performance." Jules sighs and tucks his hands into the pockets of his pants, stretching his velvet blazer across his shoulders. He glances up at the ceilings—plain and unremarkable backstage—but his eyes are dreamy. He looks exactly how I thought I would feel when we finally made it to this iconic performance hall. Instead, I'm just tired. Jules smiles again, this time softer. "What would I have to do to convince you to go out with me tonight to celebrate?"

"If I don't remove these torture devices masquerading as shoes in the next five minutes, I might actually die. Which would be terribly inconvenient for our record label."

He chuckles but his gaze skims down me, slowly, before it lands on my feet. Then he drags his emerald eyes back up to meet mine. "At least let me bring champagne to your room. We should mark the occasion properly. After all, it's our last performance together for a while unless you've reconsidered Vienna."

I take a slow breath. The air backstage is cool and almost metallic, filled with the waxy smells of polished wood and freshly applied rosin. "I haven't. But I need a break, Jules. I'm taking a sabbatical."

He shifts his violin case. "A break without your favorite

duet partner?" His voice is light, but a wrinkle has formed between his brows. "What about the album?"

I reach out and clasp his hand which causes the tension in his shoulders to ease. "It's not about us or the album. I'll continue composing and we can coordinate virtually. We live in a global world, don't we? I just need a chance to breathe."

"You breathe when you play," he whispers, then his voice rises in volume again. "You breathe when we make music. You've said that yourself."

I had. Music had once been like breathing to me. When we started this tour nine months ago—it somehow got extended by three months and I'd somehow agreed—I'd practically pranced into every music hall with stage lights dancing in my eyes.

But I'm exhausted now.

"I want a chance to visit my sister."

"Wait, you're planning to take your sabbatical in *Maple Grove*?"

"Magnolia Cove." I heft my cello and walk down the hall. "You know the name."

He hustles after me, and we weave past stage crew in their all black outfits. "Of course I remember Magnolia Cove. The place you disappeared to for a week last summer and had zero cell reception."

I reach my changing room but turn to face him, the cool metal of the door handle grounding me. "Exactly. When I say I need to breathe, that's what I mean. I want to see my sister and I want to take a break in a place where I can hear music again —real music. Not the roar of an audience or the endless echo of a critic's verdict."

Jules actually appears baffled for a minute, his brow furrowing in a comical way. It's strange to see him like that. He's usually the picture of confidence—pressed collars, perfect posture, and a quip ready on his lips. "That roar means we've done something extraordinary, Missy. Together, we're... we're two of the most precise, technically proficient performers out there. Do you know how rare that is? To find the connection we have."

My fingers drop from the handle. I know he's right. For all the differences in our personalities, there's no musician who matches me the way Jules does—not in precision, not in technical execution, not in our shared enthusiasm for complex pieces.

Neither of us is successful on our own. The tour presented us as a pair. Raised us both to stardom as a pair. If I step down from performing even for a season, I'm stepping back Jules' career as well.

"I know. I just need a chance to refill the creative well."

"Do you remember that night in Rome? When we played until sunrise?" I close my eyes because I do remember. It was a few months into the tour, when we realized what a force we were together. We played across the river from the Temple of Aesculapius until orange swept the sky and reflected in the water. My muscles trembled from exhaustion and my fingers burned, but when I lifted my face to meet Jules' intense expression, I knew I'd found my musical partner. "That's who you are. Margaret Sinclair, cellist extraordinaire. You're not meant for small towns and wedding gigs."

I pinch the bridge of my nose. "We can still finish the album and—"

"This isn't about the album." He kicks back a foot, knocking nine hundred dollar shoes against the wall. "This is about you running from everything you've built—everything we've built. I know you've felt overwhelmed with the rapid rise in celebrity and the demanding schedule. But Missy you were born for this."

"I'm not running away." The fluorescent light overhead flickers. "I just need a break."

"Since when do you need a break? You live for this. *We* live for this."

"I'm not asking you to understand." I click open the dressing room door. "And I'm not quitting or running away. I just... need this."

Something in my voice must finally reach him because his head tilts to the side, and he chews his lip—a nervous habit I've seen in countless rehearsals.

"Six months," he says finally. "And we'll work on the album virtually during that time?"

"Of course we will, Jules. The album is brilliant and maybe you can even come visit me."

He scowls but his eyes sparkle. "What is the nightlife like?"

"Non-existent." At his lips flattening, I laugh. "You never know, you might love it. It's the kind of place that grows on you."

After all, it grew on Alex. One day my sister was rising to the top of her career, writing for a prestigious food magazine, considering a senior editing position in New York City. Next she's quitting it all in order to move to an island of five thousand people and minimal internet service. And she's never been happier.

"Not likely, darling." Jules leans against the doorframe and looks down at me. "Forgive me for being so insistent. I just don't want to see you squander a talent like yours, plus I'll miss you."

"I'll miss you too. Who else is going to critique—in three different languages—the bargain-bin shoes I buy?"

He scoffs. "Perhaps if you bought quality shoes, you wouldn't describe them as torture devices."

I chuckle and realize how close we're standing. His eyes are warm in the glowing light from my dressing room, his hair curling perfectly against his forehead. He looks like a prince who stepped out of a storybook. But somehow I've never wanted to ride into the sunset with him. Maybe it's like the shoes. I'm not used to having the income to purchase expensive clothing, yet. Instead, I've tucked away most of my salary this year. But maybe in a few years I'll get there. Maybe the idea of Jules as more than just a musical partner will warm to me in the same way.

I set my cello down and wrap my arms around him. He sighs into the back of my neck and pulls me tight.

"I really will miss you, Jules."

When we pull back, he reaches up and tucks a strand of hair behind my ear. I freeze and can't decide if I want to jerk away or lean closer. Before I can choose, Jules gives a careless shrug and walks down the hall. "Keep your phone somewhere with internet connectivity if you've ever cared about me."

"I will."

Then he's gone, and I step into the dressing room and shut the door. The bulbs on the vanity cast soft, golden rings of light over everything. I drag myself across the carpeted floors and drop onto the stool. On the table sits a stack of pictures—large prints of Jules and me on stage, smiling at each other like we're the sun and moon, holding each other in perfect orbit.

There's at least forty of them, and they all need signatures. I groan but my phone that sits propped against the mirror buzzes. Alex's name pops up alongside an emoji of a croissant and a pencil.

I let it ring for a minute. Take a deep, grounding breath.

Because if there's anything I won't do, it's show my misery to my sister. She sacrificed too much to get me where I'm at. She's always downplayed it, but I know she gave up most of her twenties getting me through college debt-free. Now I'm making six figures following the dream she sacrificed to make happen. I refuse to express anything but deep gratitude and to be anything other than Alex's playful, happy younger sister.

With a swipe, the screen comes to life and Alex and Ethan's smiles fill the frame. Their faces distort and freeze for a second before coming back to life again. Magnolia Cove really does have terrible cell service.

"Hi, sis! How did the last performance go?"

"Standing ovation. Jules was brilliant, as always."

Ethan gives one of his massive grins. "If I know anything, my sister-in-law shined as well."

"I agree." Alex is practically beaming, her fingers tucked under chin. Her engagement ring glimmers even over the pixelated video footage. "We should have flown to see this one!"

"What? Are you kidding?" I laugh, forcing the expression even though it feels like the most contrived one I've worn all week. "You already saw the show in Paris and Milan."

"And both were brilliant." Ethan sighs wistfully and looks at my sister. "Not to mention the boulangeries and pâtisseries we got to visit."

"Perfection." She nudges him. "I still think your pain au chocolat outshines any we've had along the Seine, though."

The way Alex looks at Ethan—like he's her entire world wrapped in flour and sugar—makes my chest ache with happiness for her. After everything she gave up for me, she deserves this kind of love. This kind of contentment.

"Actually..." I twist a loose strand of hair around my finger. "I was thinking about taking my sabbatical in Magnolia Cove. Maybe help with the wedding planning some?"

The video image freezes at that moment, capturing Alex and Ethan's parting lips and raised eyebrows. They don't want me to come. Of course, they probably want to spend this time alone and I'd just burden them.

"Or not. I could always go back to New York and—"

"Of course we'd love for you to come, Missy." The video unfreezes and Alex and Ethan exchange a meaningful look before my sister turns back toward me. "Magnolia Cove is just kind of weird about long-term visitors."

"I can rent a place. I have the money."

Alex laughs. "I'd hope you'd stay with us, of course. You just kind of need permission to stay longer than a month."

"Permission?" They exchange another look. I chew my lip. "Alex, blink twice if you're in a cult and need rescuing."

"No cult. Nothing that exciting, I'm afraid." Alex swipes golden bangs back from her forehead. "It's just... the town council is really strict about residency permits. Something about preserving the island's character and limited housing. But don't worry—Ethan knows someone on the council. We can probably fast track your application. I'll email it to you."

Ethan frowns at my sister. "I know someone on the council?"

She raises her eyebrows. "Yes."

A sigh escapes my brother-in-law, and he scrubs a hand over his face before nodding. "Don't worry about it, Missy. We'll get it taken care of." His expression softens as he smiles at Alex again. "I know your sister will love having you visit for a while longer."

His tone puts me at ease. Okay, they're happy to see me. And I'll make sure I'm not a burden, starting with filling out this application to perfection so they don't have to correct anything.

"Sounds great. I'll see you guys next week, then?"

"See you then!" The video freezes again, their faces paused in bright, happy expressions.

All right, Magnolia Cove. Here I come.

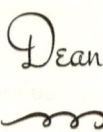

Dean

I've decided I hate the color cream.

I can't stop rotating the damned envelope that arrived this morning and ruined my daily agenda. It's cream, of course. Heavy for a letter. Closed with a golden seal.

And it's from my family.

Mom called on Sunday like she does every week. Months have passed since she sent me mail. But it's not even her name on the envelope. It's Nell's.

I flip it over again.

Feel the weight of it in my hand.

A dozen magical crises happened just last month, and I didn't hesitate a beat. Wielding enough magic that I cause most people—humans and magical types alike—to veer away from me? Standard Monday. Helping infuse the heavy wards required to keep the magic in a tourist destination like Magnolia Cove under wraps? Piece of cake. Dealing with shifters or warlocks who lose control of their magic? Nothing a massage won't fix.

But one letter from my sister and I might as well be nine-teen again. Breaking my sister's heart. Making a choice that would split our family and cause me to leave home forever and move to Magnolia Cove.

Sitting here in this office, I'm ignoring a dozen magical inquiries, half a dozen wards that need inspection, a lunch meeting about the Harvest Hoopla, and—because the universe has a sense of humor—a request to approve another human for long-term residency. Another Sinclair sister. Perfect. Because what this town really needs is one more human who sees too much.

I reach for the medallion I've carried since graduating from Calthorne—one of the few magical universities that actually matters. The crest is worn smooth, but the weight is the same. It's a reminder of everything it took to shoulder this kind of responsibility. Enough power to hold a town's wards steady. Enough training to manage its magic safely. Enough control to do it without burning everything down. I've gone hand to... well, paw with werewolves and bear shifters and didn't blink. But I can't bring myself to open this damn envelope.

It's now one of the two personal items in the room. The other is a picture I never look at. Otherwise I keep my office sparse. Nothing hangs on the marbled emerald and ebony walls. The recessed bookshelves hold all the standard magical law texts—*The Codex Arcanum*, *The Charter of the Council*, and *Binding Principles of Magic*. There's a dusty set of various years' copies of The Mage's Code of Conduct. My ledger— heavily warded—and my Parker Duofold Centennial fountain pen sit on the desk's polished wood.

And now the letter.

Which I can't force myself to open.

A set of heavy knocks on the door pull me out of my stupor. "It's open," I say as I stand and shove the envelope into my leather jacket's inside pocket.

Eleanor pokes her head inside, the wrinkles at her eyes

more pronounced than normal. As head of the local council—and my second in command—she doesn't waste time with pleasantries. "Dean, we have a problem."

Of course we do.

We always have a problem.

I bob my head and follow her out.

* * *

The crowd outside Petal Pushers is dense. Eleanor and I make our way up Main Street and its perfectly maintained cobblestone road. Oaks draped in Spanish moss and Magnolia trees stretch overhead, casting the entire downtown in cool, dappled shade. The crowd parts before us—mostly tourists, phones raised high, capturing what they think is some quaint small-town attraction.

If only they knew.

Mums and marigolds pirouette in their ceramic pots, showering the air with sparkly golden pollen that catches the dappled sunlight filtering through leaves. The display would be almost beautiful if it weren't so dangerous. Magic ripples through the air, making my teeth ache.

My fellow council members—all powerful witches and warlocks—already work the crowd. There are seven of us total, appointed by the National Council after the usual trials and tests. I'm Head Warlock here—part political figure, part magical janitor. Depends on the day. I catch Gerald's eye and he nods, understanding my silent command. Start with the phones. Then the memories. Gentle touches only. Memory magic leaves scars if one isn't careful.

"Can we book this for my daughter's wedding?" A tourist has cornered Iris, the shop's owner who stands against the wall like the woman in her beach cover up is wielding a weapon instead of a question. "Is there a waiting list?"

I resist the urge to clench my fists as I step beside them. "It's experimental technology. Not available for private events."

I reach out with my magic. Gentle. Careful. Find the edges of the last ten minutes and blur them softly, like morning mist rolling over the sea. Her pupils dilate as the magic takes hold. The wonder in her eyes fades and she furrows her brow.

"I'm sorry." She blinks then looks around. "What was I asking about?"

"The Harvest Hoopla," I lie smoothly. "It's our big fall festival in a few weeks. Plenty of local vendors will be there."

She nods and drifts away, already forgetting our conversation. I watch her go, tasting mint and regret on my tongue— the lingering almost painfully spicy signature of memory magic that will grow until it burns my sinuses and causes my eyes to water. I've always hated memory magic, the physical discomfort of using it being the least reason.

Most magic has limits, but not consequences. Infusing comfort into baked goods or small protection wards all hum along harmlessly, like a current that knows its path.

But high-level magic like the kind I wield always comes with a cost. It wears you down—in your bones, in your thoughts, in the way you sleep at night. The greater the spell, the more it takes.

And very few people are built to handle it. Not just magically, but mentally. Emotionally. There's a reason most burn out early or lose themselves along the way. To wield this kind of power and stay intact takes discipline. Distance.

"Dean," Iris breathes. She's shaking so much her ivory hair trembles and she clutches her arms around herself. "I didn't know. The performance was supposed to be simple... just a few students and—"

"Everything's under control." I keep my voice level despite the headache building behind my eyes. "Your shop's reputation won't suffer; we'll make sure of it. Everything will be back to normal in a few hours."

"But the tourists—"

"Won't remember anything unusual." I soften my tone. A few years back when someone accidentally turned all her roses neon green she'd cried. "We'll handle it."

Her lip wobbles but she gives me a nod.

That's my role here—handling things. Cleaning up messes. Keeping everyone safe, even if they sometimes resent my methods. The weight of their reliance settles across my shoulders like a familiar coat. Heavy, but perfectly tailored.

Let them whisper about the stern council member, the one who has lived here nearly a decade and hasn't integrated into the Cove's social life. Let them think I'm cold, unapproachable. It's easier that way. Clean. Like magical theory— every action has an equal reaction. Stay distant, stay focused, and problems get solved without the messy complications of emotional entanglement.

The envelope in my pocket from my family seems to burn my chest. That's what brought me here in the first place. Caring too much, getting tangled up and hesitating instead of doing what needed to be done. That led to the problem becoming massive and the hurt mirroring it in size.

Never again. Some lessons leave scars that remind you why walls are necessary. I straighten my jacket, brush away the dusting of pollen over its smooth black surface.

Rachel, a local music teacher, stands protectively in front of her student—Emma, the young witch who started this mess. The girl clutches her violin case like a shield, trembling. This isn't our first conversation about magic this year. Three times I've had to pull her aside after incidents at school. A shattered window when she got frustrated with a difficult passage. Wind that howled through the halls during her solo at the spring concert. Now this. The girl has power thrumming through her veins like a crescendo building to its peak, raw and wild and dangerous. Her extra lessons with Rachel aren't helping as much as I'd hoped they would.

I recognize that particular brand of untamed magic. The way it builds under your skin like a storm gathering force, how it begs for release, for expression. At her age, I shattered more than windows. Created tempests that made today's sparkly pollen show look like a gentle spring shower.

It took years for me to learn to control my magic. To learn the costs of having it.

I walk toward them. Rachel meets me halfway, her nose flaring. "Before you start, she was just trying to take part in a normal school activity."

"Normal?" The word tastes bitter. "Normal doesn't usually involve enchanted horticulture."

"We can't deny her regular experiences just because—"

"Just because she could expose our entire community?" Pollen settles once again on my black jacket. I brush it off with more force than needed. I'm going to have to break out the microfiber cloth and leather conditioner tonight, though. "She needs control first. Then performances."

Every time magic slips into the open anywhere in the world it's the magical community that pays the price. Fear makes people dangerous, and history's been painfully consistent on that point. Salem comes to mind. Hundreds of innocent people—mostly non-magical humans—lost their lives, and the fallout laid the groundwork for the council system we have now.

I wait in silence until finally Rachel sighs and steps out of my way. All of us have had moments of wishing we weren't born magical, but we also all have to come to terms with what we are at some point too.

"Go easy on her," Rachel says as I pass. "It wasn't intentional."

I gesture for Emma to follow me to a quieter spot near the alley. She does, her violin case bumping her legs.

"I didn't mean to," she whispers. "The magic just felt so..."

"Powerful." I finish for her. I'd had many similar moments in my past. "Yes, I know. But that's exactly why you need to learn control first."

"I don't want control." She still trembles but she juts her chin up, causing her tight dark curls to spill over her shoulder. "I don't want magic at all. Music is what I love and what I'm good at. I want to go to Juilliard and—"

"Juilliard won't be possible if you can't manage your magic." Her face crumples and my stomach twists. But I remember the cost of unleashing that much raw magic without control. What it destroys. Who it hurts. And how long it takes to rebuild afterward—if you can rebuild at all. I remember Nell's tears. "You have extraordinary potential, Emma. As a musician and a witch. But with that comes responsibility."

She bows her head and clutches the violin even tighter. "I'm sorry. I won't let it happen again."

She probably will, but I know she means her words. "All right, then. Better get back to your teacher. I think she's worried about you."

The girl scurries away, and I exhale slowly, trying to steady the energy still buzzing in the air. My hand slips into my pocket, reaching for the familiar weight of the medallion I always carry, but instead, my fingers brush paper.

The envelope.

I pull it out before I can talk myself out of it. The seal breaks easily under my thumb.

An invitation, as expected. Cream card stock, gold lettering. Nell is getting married. That leaves me unsteady on my feet for a moment. I don't even know who my sister is marrying. I don't even know my sister anymore. But it's the note from my mother that makes my throat tight.

Dean,

We miss you. All of us. I know you probably won't come, but we had to try. Maybe it's time to heal these old wounds. Please attend Nell's wedding. Let us try to be a family again.

Love,

Mom

I trace the words, the slight indentations her pen left in the paper scraping my finger. Around me, Magnolia Cove hums with contained magic, with secrets and responsibilities. With the weight of choices made and prices paid.

The envelope slips back into my pocket. Some wounds aren't meant to heal. Some distances must be maintained. Because some actions are unforgivable. Even if maintaining that means standing alone.

Always alone.

Missy

The ferry's horn blasts in the distance, but I barely notice. My entire walk down Main Street felt unusually lonely. A first in Magnolia Cove. Then I spot the crowd, all drawn to the same thing: autumn flowers outside a shop, their petals swaying as if dancing to a rhythm only they could hear. They shimmer with something that looks like dewdrops caught in the sunrise. The display reminds me of that moment in a performance when technical precision gives way to pure feeling, when music transcends its written boundaries to become something alive, something magic.

Even when the flowers stop their movement and the crowd drifts away, I can't shake the sensation that I've witnessed something extraordinary. Something that exists in the liminal space between what's possible and what's real, like the pause between movements in a concerto—pregnant with possibility and anticipation.

My phone buzzes. Again. Because apparently while everyone else on the island struggles to get a single bar of service, my phone has decided its gift in life is getting just enough coverage to receive Jules' increasingly dramatic emails.

I shift my cello case, trying to dig the device from my pocket without dropping either my backpack or the instrument that's worth more than most cars.

The wind picks up, carrying more of the golden pollen from the flowers. Their petals droop toward the soil, edges curling like they've been out in the sun too long. Even the stems seem to sag, barely holding themselves upright. I breathe in right as pollen reaches me and—

"Achoo!"

The sneeze catches me off guard in its intensity, causing me to tumble forward. My cello case tilts precariously as I lose my grip, and my heart stops. Six figures of handcrafted Italian craftsmanship about to meet concrete. I will literally throw my entire body to the ground as a cushion if that's what it takes. Bruises heal, instruments don't, and—

Strong hands catch me mere inches from disaster. The momentum spins us both, and suddenly I'm pressed against a solid chest, looking up into dark eyes that remind me of coffee grounds in morning light. He's wearing all black, which should look severe but instead makes him seem substantial somehow, like he's carved from shadow and certainty.

"Oh, I..." More sparkly pollen drifts between us. I scrunch my nose, a tickle spreading like a feather brushing the back of my throat. I try to fight but it wins. "Ah...achoo!"

This time I sneeze directly in his face.

It's not one of those delicate, socially acceptable sneezes. No, this is the kind that starts somewhere around your ankles and builds like a crescendo, the sort that would make my old conductor wince and mark it fortissimo. The kind that probably registers on local seismographs.

All the blood rushes away from my face and my mouth flies open. I want to cover it with my hands but my arms are still captured in his firm embrace. He blinks, a few sparkles clinging to his dark eyelashes. A muscle ticks in his jaw and I can't tell if he's angry or trying not to laugh. Probably angry, given how his presence seems to radiate authority like heat from summer pavement.

If this is any sign how my sabbatical will go, I should start composing my own requiem now. First movement: "The Cellist Who Died of Embarrassment After Sneezing on the Town's Most Handsome Man." Second movement: "Why Does Gravity Betray Musicians?" The final movement would be six minutes of awkward silence, punctuated by occasional sneezing.

But there's something about the way he's looking at me—a flicker of humanity beneath his carefully composed expression—that makes me pause my mental composition.

"I'm so sorry," I manage. The blood has returned to my face and burns across my cheeks. "I swear I'm not usually in the habit of assaulting strangers with projectile germs."

Oh god. I just said that out loud. To this beautiful man.

His lips turn up at one corner and those dark eyes haven't slipped away from me once. He releases me slowly, like he wants to make sure I'm truly steady before letting me go. "Good to know should we meet again I won't feel the temptation to cross the street and use the other sidewalk."

A group of official-looking people have surrounded the flower shop. Their behavior, the way they whisper to each other, is odd. When I shift my attention back to my rescuer he's studying me with an intensity that reminds me of my first Juilliard audition—that feeling of being deconstructed note by note, evaluated for both technical precision and something deeper, less definable.

I see the intimidation his appearance must offer others. Though he smells amazing—like autumn leaves, wood smoke, and cinnamon. If others got this close to him, they might feel as intrigued as I do. But I somehow doubt anyone does. He just has that aura about him.

"Thank you for saving Giuseppe." I pat my cello case. "He's irreplaceable."

One dark eyebrow lifts. "You named your cello Giuseppe?"

"Don't judge. He's Italian and temperamental. It fits."

A muscle in his jaw ticks. I'm almost certain he's suppressing amusement. Golden light catches on his cheekbones as he studies me with an intensity that should be uncomfortable but instead feels... interesting. Like being the subject of a particularly thorough composition.

"You're watching the flowers," he says, his tone shifting to something more hoarse, darker.

"Oh. Yes." I glance back at the strange dance. "They were quite... lively. Magnolia Cove and its surprises, am I right?" I grin up at him. He doesn't return it and I immediately feel like I've just played "Hot Cross Buns" at Carnegie Hall. Perfectly executed, completely inappropriate, and impossible to recover from with dignity.

"Other tourists have moved on." The man's intensity has grown. The shift in the air between us is electric. It's the same feeling I get before a difficult performance—that awareness of standing on the edge of something that requires perfect precision to navigate correctly. His gaze shifts to Giuseppe, then narrows. What kind of vendetta could anyone have against a cello?

"Guess I'm the special nosy and particularly stubborn variety." I straighten my posture. I don't know who this man thinks he is, but I've made a career in a world where nearly all the leadership positions are held by men who think their batons are extensions of their egos. His intensity might be greater than most, but I've faced down maestros who think they're directing the second coming of Beethoven. He might have gorgeous dark eyes and a jawline sharp enough to cut glass, but he doesn't scare me. I shift my cello case. "Though if you're planning to write me up for unauthorized flower-watching, I should warn you Giuseppe has excellent credentials as a character witness."

A flicker of a smile ghosts across his face, gone almost as quickly as it appears. "Unauthorized flower-watching isn't typically a punishable offense." His gaze flicks briefly to Giuseppe, then back to me. "Though, I'll admit, I've never had a cello act as someone's legal counsel before. I guess that makes you... unique."

"The uniquest." I offer him the smile I've used to charm grumpy conductors, skeptical donors, and the occasional overzealous critic. His expression doesn't shift—much—but there's a sparkle to his eye that tells me another story. "Actually, maybe you can help me?" I shift Giuseppe's weight and fish out the wrinkled paper I'd scribbled Alex's directions onto earlier. "Maybe you could point me in the right direction. I'm supposed to talk with someone named Dean Markham?"

His posture, already straight, somehow becomes even straighter. "You already are."

"Oh." I look him over again—the authority, the all-black outfit, the careful control. Of course he's the bureaucrat Alex warned me about. "Well, that's... efficient."

"Indeed. Margaret Sinclair, I presume. You can come with me."

I groan but fall in step beside him, dragging Giuseppe along like a reluctant accomplice. Of course I'd sneeze in the face of the person who has to approve my residency permit.

Dean

Alex Sinclair's sharp heels announce her arrival before she bursts through my door, all pressed angles and indignation. Her sister turns toward her and offers a wave. They resemble each other in some ways—the gold-streaked hair and high cheekbones. But Margaret stands out with her warm curves, soft curls, and golden eyes that sparkle with humor. It's a striking contrast to Alex's sharp, no-nonsense journalistic demeanor. While Alex is all edges and focus, Margaret seems to invite the world in with a tilt of her head. The woman who sneezed in my face not twenty minutes ago. Who felt like possibilities when I caught her. Who named her cello Giuseppe.

I'm no stranger to desire; the occasional trysts at The National Council of Witches and Warlocks biennial meetings serve their purpose. Discreet encounters with people who understand the value of distance. But this... this feels different.

I shift my fingers, brushing the edge of the medallion in my pocket. The envelope presses against it, a silent weight reminding me exactly why I don't do this. Don't let myself feel this electric awareness of another person. Especially when that other person is a non-magical human.

"Did you detain my sister at the ferry?" Alex slams her fists against her hips and glares. She doesn't even realize she has the ability to do this—to remind everyone that she once worked in Manhattan boardrooms and fears nothing.

I'm still tasting mint and regret from the memory magic I had to perform on the tourist crowd. My sinuses burn, my head pounds, and now this complication walks into my office.

I rest my elbows on my desk and press my fingers together. "I'm just following the procedure for extended-stay visitors, Ms. Sinclair. You know this."

"Then why didn't you inform me first and—"

"Actually, the ferry arrived early." Her sister's voice is soft, musical even in speech. "I thought I'd walk down and meet you. Mr. Markham was kind enough to escort me here."

"Dean," I correct automatically, then immediately regret giving her that familiarity. The smile that curves her lip suggests she plans to use it against me—like I just handed her a secret and she can't wait to see how far she can push it.

"Dean, I mean." Her gaze stays locked on mine for two heartbeats too long. It's electric, so powerful it overrides the magic-induced headache. She turns back to her sister and grasps her hands. "Everything's fine. I'll meet you at your restaurant when I'm done?"

"Well..." Alex's sharp glance fixes back on me before returning to Margaret. "I can stay for the interview if you'd like."

"I'm fine." She shrugs. "What do I have to hide?"

Alex tenses, her fingers tightening around Margaret's. At least she's aware of the issue. *She* may have nothing to hide, but *we* do. Decades of careful magical concealment wrapped in small town charm and council regulations.

I tap my fingers together, the motion reflecting in my

desk's polished mahogany. "I believe, Ms. Sinclair, I've given you reason for faith in the past."

Alex's lips thin. She holds my stare like her sister did, but it feels completely different. Like a challenge. Magic rises unbidden beneath my skin, an instinctive response to confrontation—one I've spent years learning to control.

Emma's defiant jut of her jaw from this morning comes to mind—how she clutched her violin case like a shield even as raw power hummed over her skin. I recognize that brand of magic. The kind that doesn't ask for permission or wait for convenient moments. The kind that builds like a storm until it breaks through every barrier you try to construct.

Of course, I never longed to leave the magical community as she does. Never wanted to leave home.

I swear the envelope is stabbing me in the ribs.

Some lessons carve themselves into bone. You learn to contain magic, or it contains you. You master control, or you lose everything that matters.

And that's why, despite the power, it's easy to swallow the magic down and give Alex a terse smile.

"Fine," she mutters, then turns to her sister and embraces her before kissing her cheek.

When the door clicks shut, Margaret doesn't take a seat like a normal person. Instead, she flashes that dangerous grin at me once more before casually strolling around the office. She lifts her face at the expanse of the bookshelf, grazes a finger over one book's spine, then pauses at *The Codex Arcanum*, disguised as a mundane legal text.

My magic prickles beneath my skin as her fingers drift closer to its spelled binding. Every protective instinct I possess wants to stop her, to preserve the careful order I've built here, but something about her deliberate exploration holds me silent.

Watching her, I can imagine her playing the cello that

currently leans in its case against a corner alongside her suit-case. I can imagine her grip tightening around the bow, her body swaying with the music, those graceful fingers drawing out notes like she's pulling magic from the strings. I shift in my seat because I don't understand this magnetic attraction I feel toward her and I don't like things I can't explain.

Margaret's hand drops. She looks back over her shoulder like she can feel my discomfort. With a shift of her hips that twirls her dress around her legs, she walks over to the desk. Those graceful fingers reach out again, pausing before touching the silver-framed photo I keep faced away.

"Oh, you have a sister too."

The mint taste of memory magic strengthens again and turns bitter. I open a drawer to find a cinnamon-flavored mint to pop into my mouth. Anything to rid myself of this lingering taste of the past.

"I'm not the one being interviewed."

She grins and settles into the chair across from me, all graceful movements but her eyes promise mischief.

I pull out the form and lift my pen. "So what exactly brings you to Magnolia Cove?"

I need to get through these questions as efficiently as possible and get this woman out of my office and preferably my life—quickly.

She tilts her head, studying me like I'm something worth looking at. No one has looked at me like that in years—like I'm someone they want to understand rather than avoid. The back of my neck prickles as she speaks.

"Besides my sister's upcoming wedding?" A pause occurs while she whirls a ring on her pinky finger. "Well, there's this grumpy bureaucrat who seemed like he could use someone to practice his scowling on and that feels like a noble use of my sabbatical time." She smirks. "You're doing great, by the way.

Very intimidating. Do you rehearse your expression in the mirror?"

"Miss Sinclair—"

"Missy," she interrupts smoothly, her grin widening. "Since we're on a first-name basis now, Dean."

She says my name like she's tasting it, like it's a piece of music she's considering how to play. The electric feeling increases. I'm certain if I reach out to touch the paper now, a static shock would leap up and shock me.

She twirls a strand of golden hair around her finger. "Besides, you're deflecting. You've avoided my question about if you practice in the mirror." She leans forward and whispers. "You can tell me. I'm great at keeping secrets."

"You also seem to excel at sneezing in strangers' faces."

A whisper of red washes over her nose but she falls back into a chair with a laugh. "I'm a woman of many talents, Dean."

And that's exactly what I'm afraid of. The way she notices too much, asks too many questions, and already seems to draw toward anything radiating with magic. Like me.

The magic under my skin pulses. It's becoming so untethered it should throb in my temples and ache into my bones, but it's not. It's simply rushing through me, like it's responding to her presence, even though she's a regular human. Or maybe because she is one. The dangerous ones always are—the ones who can peer through our carefully constructed illusions, who find the cracks in our magical concealment. After all, her sister had done the same.

"And," she says, "you still haven't answered."

I think of Emma's raw power this morning, of Nell's broken heart a decade ago, and clear my throat. "Anything done with excellence requires practice." I deadpan the response but she smiles, anyway. Without taking a breath I continue, "You're planning to stay for how long?"

Her eyes are warm honey when they meet mine. She looks at me straight in the face—the way even most witches and warlocks won't. "That depends. How long does it usually take to make you crack a smile? Because now it's become a personal challenge."

Her fingers dance against her armrest. I track the motion, their rhythm and sway. A shiver slips down my spine and I force my gaze back down to the blank page.

"Your touring partner, Jules Bouchard..." Her smile drops and her eyebrows rise and I'm pleased to have surprised her. "Will he visit during your stay?"

A shadow settles over her expression and she finally shifts those intense eyes away. "Not likely. Jules isn't exactly the small-town type."

"And you are?"

A dangerous question. An unnecessary question. Yet, I can't regret asking it.

She meets my gaze again. "I could be."

The air thickens with unspoken meaning. In another life, with different choices, this might have led somewhere else. I've seen that expression before—dim corners, whispered invitations—but this is different. There's something genuine in how she holds my gaze, how she says my name like a gift instead of a conquest.

If I were someone else—someone without regrets, without past mistakes—I might lean closer. I might learn if her laugh feels as musical up close as it does across the room.

But I am who I am. Head Warlock of Magnolia Cove. Keeper of secrets. Already destroyer of one sister's happiness. And she is who she is—human, perceptive, dangerous.

Some doors are better left unopened. Some songs better left unplayed.

I clear my throat and straighten the still-blank forms that don't need straightening.

"Six months," she whispers, breaking the quiet. "My sabbatical is for six months."

I scribble the number down. Ask a few more to-the-point questions. Then I rise. "Your application will need council review. I'll contact you with their decision."

She stands as well and smooths her dress. "Thank you, Dean." The smirk slides back onto her lips. "I look forward to giving you more opportunities to practice that scowl."

I offer her a curt nod and she gathers her bags and leaves, clicking the door shut behind her. I'm certain she's going to give me plenty of opportunities, because every moment in her presence is an exercise in restraint. It's taking all my energy not to lean closer when she speaks, not track the graceful arch of her neck when her hair spills away from it, not let my power reach for her like a flower turning toward the sun.

I wait until her footsteps fade before moving to the window. Outside she reunites with Alex who waited for her. They embrace then head toward town. Something within me wants to ask her to return, wants to keep hearing her voice, move my chair to sit beside hers, hope we might touch.

"No." I'm not in a habit of speaking aloud to myself, but this moment feels like it requires the weight of sound. "Absolutely not."

I pull the blinds shut and return to my desk. I'm not giving in to attraction for a non-magical human—or anyone, for that matter. Love leads to heartbreak. To the bitter taste of necessary cruelty. To a sister who never forgives you for doing what had to be done.

I fish the wedding invitation out. The cream color is dull in the room's dim light. Nell's name gleams up at me. Accusing me.

I reach for another mint. Pop it in my mouth. Roll it between my teeth.

Missy's honey-warm eyes linger in my memory, refusing

dismissal. The way magic has an aftertaste so that you have to keep remembering it long after the moment has passed.

The form sits before me, waiting for decisions that shouldn't be this difficult. Everyone on the council likes and trusts Alex and Ethan. This interview was a formality. But the final decision rests on me.

Six months.

Six months of having her in Magnolia Cove, of crossing paths with her in the streets, of being the one called if things go wrong and she realizes too much. Six months of fighting this pull like gravity, like magic, like fate.

I reach for my pen and let it dangle above the paper. I already know how the council will vote. But they still need my signature.

A moment passes. Nell's name stares at me. I close my eyes and remember Missy's laugh, the electricity between us.

With a sigh, I open my eyes again, and let my signature glide across the page.

Missy

The scent of garlic and herbs fills Alex's cottage so thoroughly I'm sure I'll still breathe it while I sleep tonight. It reminds me of living in our apartment together, how it always smelled like gourmet restaurant leftovers or some new recipe Alex tried.

I walk toward the cutting board where a pile of washed leeks sit and eye the knife. I've never been much of a chef, but I've watched Alex enough. I think.

Before I can make that potentially reckless decision she swoops up beside me and gives me a gentle nudge. "You're my guest. Go relax."

I hover anyway, watching her efficient movements. There's a new confidence in how she handles the knife, a sureness I don't remember from our cramped apartment kitchen when dinner was whatever we could cobble together between her jobs and my practice sessions.

Now she moves like she has all the time in the world. Her once permanently furrowed brow is relaxed, and she sips at a glass of wine as she glides between the stove and the cutting board.

"At least let me set the table?" I ask.

"Already done." Ethan appears with a stack of fresh towels in hand. He drops a kiss on Alex's temple as he passes. They move around each other with the grace of dancers who've memorized their partner's rhythms.

The kitchen is compact. With me in it, I feel constantly in the way. But Ethan and Alex navigate the space like it was built for them, their movements a duet I'm not part of. It's beautiful to watch—my sister who used to rush through life with the frantic energy of someone always running late, now moving with this serene confidence. The Alex who counted every penny for my tuition would never have hummed along to the record Ethan started in the living room while she lazily chopped vegetables. She wouldn't have had time for it.

I hover to the side, my hands empty. I press them together as if that will make them less awkward and lacking.

"You can open the wine," Ethan suggests gently, as if he can read my thoughts. Then he smirks as he raises his voice to include Alex. "Tom's bringing his 'special' vintage and we'll need backup options."

Alex snorts a laugh as she scrapes the contents of her cutting board into a sizzling pan. I accept the bottles and head toward the table. Wedding magazines are stacked near the couch, a glaring reminder of everything Alex should be focusing on—planning her wedding, juggling work deadlines, managing her restaurant—anything but hosting me.

I pull a cork free from a bottle and set it with a clink against the table. Alex spent a decade putting off her dreams to support mine. Now here I am again, taking up space in a life she's finally built for herself, disrupting the careful composition of her happiness with my discordant presence.

My stomach twists, and the next bottle of wine nearly slips from my hand. Maybe I should've followed Jules, traveled more, poured everything into the album. But the thought of that dries out my mouth. Because that version of success—the constant spotlight, the airports, the interviews, the need to perform even offstage—it's perfect for someone like Jules.

But not for me.

I smack my lips and move on to the next cork.

Alex and Ethan's laughter rings out from the kitchen. I'm just going to have to find some way to make myself useful and busy for the next six months so I'm not a burden to them.

The house fills gradually with voices and laughter. Mia and Zoe arrive first, bearing a spiced rosemary and candied orange cake that spurs Ethan into asking half a dozen questions about flour grade and technique. Tom follows with his promised wine, then Violet, and finally Rachel and Grant. They all embrace me as though they've known me forever even though I'm meeting a few of them in person for the first time.

There's something fascinating about watching the group together—like observing a long-running orchestra where everyone knows their part by heart. Inside jokes flow as freely as the wine, and I smile even when I don't quite get the references. Even Alex seems to slide into their dynamic like she's been part of it all along.

"So..." Rachel leans forward, her second glass of wine nearly drained. "Are we finally going to discuss the elephant in the room?" She grins at Alex. "Will your incredibly talented sister provide the wedding music?"

Heat floods my cheeks. And it's another reminder that I can't quit my life. Alex has sacrificed so much to make it happen and she's so damn proud of me for it. She looks over the emptied plates and gleaming glasses at me and her brow furrows. Her lips part, probably to excuse away her friend's request. *Don't worry about it, Missy. Of course I have a plan.*

"I'd love to," I chime in, before she says anything. "If you'd like that. I draw the line at *Wagner's Wedding March*, however."

"Thank god," Ethan mutters, then brightens. "Speaking

of the wedding, Zoe, I was thinking maybe you could be an actual guest this time? Let someone else handle the pastries and cake?"

Zoe's fork clatters against her plate. She jerks her head up so quickly the purple in her hair catches the light, shimmering like a prism. "I'm sorry, did you suggest serving subpar pastries at the wedding of not one, but two pastry chefs?"

"It's our wedding," Ethan says. "We should get to enjoy it."

"I mean..." Alex's eyes flit away from me toward Zoe. "We have other friends in the industry."

"But none from Magnolia Cove." Zoe wiggles her eyebrows like that means something special and everyone laughs like they get it. I release a breathy chuckle but have zero idea what she's referencing. Zoe punches Ethan in the arm. "You'll enjoy it best if your cake is perfect. Besides, if your future sister-in-law is providing some of the finest musical talent that recently toured the grandest performance halls in Europe, the least I can do is match that with world-class pastry."

"Speaking of romance..." Tom exchanges a knowing look with Violet. "Nothing beats a wedding trope."

"Oh god, I love weddings in books!" Violet curls her hands together, then nudges me. "Hey, maybe you'll fall in love and end up staying in Magnolia Cove too. We have a track record for that sort of thing."

Dean's face flashes unbidden through my mind—the intensity of his dark eyes, the way his presence seems to charge the air like the moment before thunder breaks. The thought catches me off guard, like hitting an unexpected note in a familiar piece. I take a sip of wine, but my pulse has picked up tempo.

"Not likely." I laugh. "I don't really have main character energy."

I've always been more comfortable offstage than in the center. Even when I'm playing, it's the music that's meant to shine—not me. I'm just the hands behind the sound.

"Besides," Mia says, "remember the last time we tried matchmaking? It was the matchmaker who fell in love, hmm. Maybe that's what you're looking for, Violet?"

"Real life romance. Eww." Violet grimaces before exchanging a high-five with Tom.

The conversation shifts into discussing Rhianna, the apparent matchmaker, and her boyfriend Eli and their recent globetrotting adventures. I chime in with thoughts on cities I've visited, soaking up the laughter and the last few bites of the delicious meal Alex and Ethan prepared. But as soon as a lull settles over the table, I excuse myself and slip out to the porch.

The ocean's rushing rhythm fills the air. A salty breeze brushes hair back from my cheeks as I lean against the railing. Dunes block the ocean's view but I've never been to a city that has stars like Magnolia Cove does. They glisten and gleam against the ebony sky like jewels.

"Mind if I join you?" Rachel walks up beside me and offers a fresh glass of wine. "Sometimes a girl needs a break from the chaos."

I accept the drink gratefully. "That obvious?"

"Just to another performer." She smiles and leans down beside me. "You know, I used to dream of touring professionally. I was never actually talented enough, but I held on to that hope for a long time. Used to imagine standing ovations, roses thrown on stage, my name in lights."

"If it helps, those lights are brutal. They make you sweat like a pig. And if you get popular enough, you have to spend the hour after an exhausting performance signing autographs until your hand cramps. It's less glorious than it sounds."

She chuckles. "Well, maybe it's good I ended up teaching.

Though sometimes managing a classroom of hormonal teenagers with instruments feels like its own struggle."

I laugh as the wine settles warm in my chest and I lean back, tension falling from my shoulders. There's something comforting about talking to another musician—someone who understands the expectations.

"I think Alex said something about you running the school's music program?"

Rachel nods and hair slips free and spills over her eyes. She bats it away. "And a summer camp. Plus private lessons for students who need extra support. You should see some of these kids. Raw talent paired with a bucket of heart. There's this one girl—Emma. She has her eyes set on Juilliard, but struggles to contain all her... umm, musical talent."

"I could help." I scarcely even notice how Rachel stumbled on the end of her words because I'm so fixed on what an obvious solution this could be. A student would spend her days in school—and I should spend that time working on compositions for mine and Jules' album. But early mornings or afternoons? I could devote hours each day to helping a promising student. She'd probably get out of school about the time the Whisk closes. It would give Ethan and Alex some alone time and get me out of their hair. I shoot up, sloshing the wine in the glass.

Rachel grimaces and gives a chuckle that sounds hollow. "I'm sure you're busy."

"Not really. I mean, I am composing, but I'd love to help a promising student, and I graduated from Juilliard. If there's anyone that could help prepare her for the stress and pressures, it would be me."

Rachel drums out a rhythm against the railing before giving a nod. "Yeah, maybe it's a good idea! Emma is... special. Incredibly gifted, but traditional conservatory training might not be the right fit. Maybe with you here for a few months though..."

Rachel's words die, and the air shifts—like the moment before a thunderstorm breaks. I don't need to turn around to know who has just walked up the path and onto the porch. Dean Markham's presence fills the space in a way that makes my skin prickle with awareness.

"Miss Sinclair." His voice is lower than I remember, rougher. I turn and my breath catches.

Memory is a poor composer. It captured the basic melody —dark eyes, strong jaw, broad shoulders. But as porch light plays across the sharp angles of his face I realize it missed all the vital harmonics that make him impossible to ignore. There's something about his persona that reminds me of the moment a conductor raises their baton—potential energy about to turn into sound.

He wears all black again, but the ocean breeze has ruffled his precise appearance. A few strands of dark hair have fallen across his forehead, and he's rolled his sleeves up to reveal forearms corded with muscle. A tremor courses through me and I realize I've been staring at him and not speaking for too long. And with an audience. An audience that's very close friends with my sister.

"Mr. Markham. Are we back to formalities?"

His expression shifts and the light glistens across his eyes, more compelling than the evening sky. He doesn't answer, just holds out a package—Jules' familiar scrawl across the front— but I'm distracted by his hands. Strong hands. Musician's hands, though I can't say how I know that.

"You deliver mail now?" I ask, the words softer than I intended.

His gaze shifts to Rachel who bobs her head to him before he answers me. "When necessary."

"This is great timing, Dean." Rachel takes a step forward.

Dean tenses, like that is his least favorite expression in an entire sea of disagreeable phrases. Even worse than 'community drum circle' or 'mandatory social gathering.' The thought of his carefully controlled reaction to those scenarios almost makes me smile. I can picture him standing ramrod straight through an impromptu karaoke session, the muscle in his jaw working overtime.

Rachel props her hands on her hips like she's up for the challenge. "I was just talking with Missy about possibly mentoring Emma—"

"No."

The word drops between us like a discordant note, sharp and jarring. Something flares in my chest—a familiar heat that reminds me of countless auctions where judges decided my fate before I played a single note. I straighten my posture, feeling the old steel of competition settle into place.

"I'm sorry," I say, not sorry at all. "But what exactly disqualifies me from teaching a student?" The wine makes me bolder, or maybe it's the way his eyes darken at my challenge. "I trained at Juilliard myself. I've toured internationally. Plus I've mentored young musicians before and—"

"This is different." His voice carries that edge of authority that probably works wonders on everyone else in town. But I've faced down conductors with god complexes and seen more of the world than this little island. Dean Markham's impressive scowl doesn't even rank in my top five of the most intimidating moments I've had with others.

Rachel jumps in front of me, like she can feel the tension building and wants to break the storm. "Dean, you know Emma needs someone who understands her desires and with Missy being Alex's sister it might be—"

"What Emma needs,"—he cuts in, and his voice has grown as dark as black diamonds—"is not up for discussion given the current circumstances."

The air has lost the easy, cool ocean breeze. It's grown charged, filled with static and I'm aware of every breath the three of us take, of the straining muscles along Dean's forearms where he's clenched his fists, of the way his gaze dips to my lips then back up to my eyes. Anger and attraction fight to propel the pulse in my chest. I can't tell which is making my heart race faster.

I'm opening my mouth to argue when the door opens and Alex walks out. The golden light from inside frames her like a spotlight, and something in her expression shifts when she takes in the scene before her—me squared off against Dean Markham, Rachel caught between us like a mediator.

"Everything okay out here?" Alex's voice carries a particular note of protectiveness I thought she'd retired after my teenage years—the tone she used with playground bullies and the unfair employer I had at my first job.

Dean's intensity banks like a fire he's carefully tamped down. "Just discussing council matters."

"Dean takes his council matters very seriously." Alex is speaking to me, I think, but her unblinking eyes remain fixed on him.

Dean frowns then looks at Rachel. "We'll discuss the situation at a more appropriate time."

Without another word, he turns and walks off the porch, disappearing into the darkness beyond the cottage light's reach. The crackling energy that surrounds him dissipates, leaving me feeling deflated.

Rachel and Alex exchange a look weighted with meaning —the kind of silent communication that comes from sharing secrets others don't understand.

Ethan's broad frame fills the doorway, blocking some of the light as he smirks at his fiancée. "I thought you said Dean wasn't so bad?" The teasing lilt in his voice only makes Alex's frown deepen.

"Maybe I'm rethinking my opinion if he's going to continue antagonizing my sister," Alex mutters, but there's something beneath her words. Something too tense for the brief interactions I've had with Dean.

Ethan presses a kiss to Alex's forehead then offers me a gentle smile. "Don't worry about Dean. He's prickly with everyone on the island."

Rachel nudges Alex. "Like a sea urchin who somehow got elected and hung around."

They both laugh and Ethan smiles down at Alex before brightening. "Speaking of prickly things, dessert's ready. Zoe's threatening to eat it all if we don't hurry."

They file back inside, Rachel squeezing my arm as she passes. I linger for a moment, drawing in a breath of the night air that still holds traces of Dean's presence—autumn leaves and thunderstorms and something darker, more magnetic. The space around me feels emptier now, a concert hall after the audience has gone and the crew has dimmed the lights.

I should be angry at Dean's dismissal, frustrated by his high-handed refusal. Instead, I'm thinking about the way his voice roughened when he said my name, how his carefully maintained control cracked just slightly when I challenged him.

I take one last breath of the autumn-scented air before turning back into the warmth and light of Alex's dinner party. But even as I step inside, I can't shake the feeling that something has shifted tonight, like the first subtle key change in what promises to be a very complicated composition.

Missy

Giuseppe and I arrive at Rachel's studio bright and early, my steps lighter than they've been in days. Whatever magic Rachel worked to change Dean's mind about me giving Emma lessons —and I'm half convinced actual magic had to be involved given his absolute refusal at the dinner party—I'm determined to prove her faith in me justified. Meeting Emma the previous afternoon went off without a hitch. She's lovely and young and excited. The familiar weight of sheet music in my arms and coffee balanced precariously in one hand feels like a possibility rather than an obligation for the first time in months.

That feeling lasts exactly as long as it takes me to push through the door into the arched golden wood room and find Dean Markham already there. Of course he is. He leans against the far wall like he's auditioning for the role of *Intimidating Authority Figure #1* in some procedural drama. Today's all-black ensemble would certainly fit the part.

Maybe Alex is right. Maybe Dean really *does* have it out for me.

I refuse to be intimidated by his presence, even if he makes the morning feel charged with... something. I'm trying to decide if that *something* is fueled more from attraction or hate as I take a breath of the sweet cedar smell permeating the room.

"Mr. Markham." I set Giuseppe against a corner. "Lost your way to the council chambers? Do city employees in Magnolia Cove not get to take a Saturday off?"

He slips a hand into his pocket and pops a breath mint into his mouth with deliberate ease, his thumb brushing the corner of his lip as he does. The movement shouldn't be compelling. It absolutely isn't compelling. "Miss Sinclair. Consider me quality control."

"For music lessons?" I straighten the sheet music and walk toward a stand.

"Among other things." Dean is in a remarkably grumpy mood this morning. Which is truly a feat considering that his standard disposition seems to hover somewhere between 'storm cloud' and 'angry cat caught in the downpour.'

I choose to ignore him and twirl around to take in the performance space. It's truly remarkable for a small music program on a little-known island. The warm wooden panels glow under soft lighting, curving gracefully overhead like the hull of an old ship turned skyward. The acoustics seem to hum with quiet anticipation, as if the room itself is holding its breath, waiting for the first note to break the silence. And Rachel told me there's several recording spaces down the far hallway as well.

"Wow," I breathe into the space, partially just to hear how my voice carries. "This place is more amazing than I expected."

That's when I realize Dean is watching me spin around beneath the wood beams and vaulted ceiling. He pushes off from the wall and steps over. With that simple movement the room feels smaller and significantly more intimate. The air between us thickens, like fog. His cologne catches me off guard for a second time. It's rich but nuanced, something you'd only notice if you got truly close to him. I somehow doubt many people get to smell it. He's near enough to touch and I've gone completely still.

"Rachel raised a great deal of money when some video went viral," he grumbles. His voice has gone low and rough but the room with its amazing acoustics brings the sound back, sending it shivering down my spine.

"Oh, I bet you just loved that." I mean for my words to come out teasing, but my tone has shifted into something soft, matching his, as if we're sharing secrets in this golden haven.

"I didn't," he whispers. The words are so faint, so close, that I can nearly imagine his breath brushing against my skin and I can't fight a shiver.

His gaze drops to my lips, lingering just a heartbeat too long. The space between us feels fragile, stretched thin by something heavier than words. I can't tell if it's the room amplifying the tension or just the undeniable *something* that crackles between us whenever we meet.

I swallow, and the sound is too loud. His eyes flick up to meet mine, and for a second, neither of us move. It's that suspended moment, like the hush before the downbeat of a symphony, when everything feels inevitable.

Dean shifts forward, just barely, and I catch my breath. I lean in, drawn as if by an invisible force. I'm barely a whisper away. From a distance his eyes appear ebony but up close they're flecked with deep amber, catching the light like sparks beneath the surface.

My gaze drops to his lips—

The door bursts open banging against the wall and light spills across the wood floors and tiered chairs.

"Hey," Rachel says then freezes mid-step, eyes flicking between us. "Am I interrupting?"

Dean clears his throat and steps back so quickly it's almost comical. "No," he says, far too fast.

I fight the urge to roll my eyes. *Subtle.* "Not at all." I walk over and open Giuseppe's case. "Perfect timing, actually."

Emma walks in, violin case in hand. Rachel doesn't even seem to notice the student's arrival as her eyebrows quirk up. "Okay, I'm going to pretend to believe that. Do you need anything before I head out? Grant and I have a pop-up ice cream stand this morning, but I can swing by later if you need me." Rachel's gaze grows in intensity. It's like she's asking me to blink twice if I need rescuing—or wink if something *else* is going on. Her eyes flick briefly to Dean, then back to me, and I resist the urge to laugh.

"I'm good. Go wow the crowds. I can handle things here."

Emma grins, oblivious to Rachel's subtle interrogation. The teen bounces on her toes. "I'll take a scoop after the lesson if you don't sell out before we're done."

Rachel smirks and wraps an arm familiarly around Emma, giving her a squeeze. "If that happens, run down to the store and tell him I said to give you a free cone on me."

"Sweet!" Emma says as Rachel gives another wave and exits. The girl's smile lingers until she notices Dean who's returned to lurking in the shadows. Her expression dims. "Oh, hi, Dean."

He nods, silent but watchful, his arms crossed as he surveys the *incredibly threatening* situation of a musician and a student preparing to tune their instruments.

"He's just here for the atmosphere." I pluck my fingers across Giuseppe's strings and hum with pleasure as the sound echoes back in the room's excellent acoustics. "Adds to the whole serious musician vibe. Venue security is part of the package for those of us who perform for a living."

Emma huffs a quiet laugh but ducks her head slightly and tucks a strand of curls behind her ear. "Yeah, sure. You're so high risk."

"Hey, give it a few years—once you're headlining, you'll

have your own Dean lurking backstage. He'll also have grumpy as his default setting and disapproval as his backup mode."

Dean's lips twitch—not quite a smile, but nearly. His eyes sparkle, though, giving him away. Maybe beneath those perfectly pressed black clothes he actually has a sense of humor. A shocking revelation. The thrill of pulling that emotion from him sings through my bones. I already want to see if I can do it again.

I lean in toward Emma and whisper, "Besides, having someone glowering at you like a cranky gnome while you play is excellent practice for becoming a performer."

A giggle escapes Emma's mouth, and she slaps her hands over her lips to try to capture the sound but does so too late.

"A gnome?" Dean sighs but his eyes still have that gleam to them. "Whispers carry in this space, and I'm still standing right here."

"Wouldn't want you anywhere else," I reply sweetly as I play a scale and nod for Emma to do the same. She lifts the violin to her chin and executes the notes perfectly.

We settle into a groove immediately—Emma playing with effortless grace, me melting into Giuseppe and swaying with the sounds, and Dean... doing whatever it is Dean does. Looming professionally, I guess.

Emma's better than I expected. When Rachel mentioned having a student who wanted to attend Juilliard I'd assumed she possessed talent, but hearing her play is something else entirely. She doesn't just perform the music, she *feels* it. That's the difference between a technician and an artist.

There's something wild and unpredictable in her performance that reminds me of myself before Juilliard polished away my rough edges. She picks up the accompaniment for "The Swan" with instinctive ease. Soon she's losing herself to the music, her hair falling across her eyes. The air seems to shift, as if it's bending to her will and—

"Emma, that's enough."

Dean's voice cuts through the music's magic, firm and low. The bow slips from Emma's strings with a jarring scrape, and she blinks as if waking from a trance.

I frown and straighten. "She was fine. Getting into the music isn't—"

I stop speaking when I see something on Dean I haven't seen before. His crossed arms aren't a show of authority—they're tight, almost tense, his fingers digging into his sleeves. His gaze isn't sharp with impatience. It's edged with something else.

Worry.

Emma doesn't argue. She lowers her violin toward its case, cheeks flushed, chest rising and falling like she's just run a mile.

"I'm good," she says quickly, brushing a sticky strand of curls off her forehead. "It's fine, Missy. Thank you. This was amazing."

Dean's jaw jumps but he nods and steps back against the wall again.

I open my mouth, ready to press the issue, but neither of them are looking at me. Whatever just happened isn't something Emma wants to explain—or Dean, for that matter.

Instead, I let out a breath, and loosen my grip on Giuseppe. "Okay, next time I'll keep a stopwatch. Apparently we have a time limit."

Emma chuckles but looks back up to me with bright eyes. "It's true that you perform with Jules Bouchard, right?"

"I do, yes. We're actually working on an album together currently."

Well, he is. My stomach twists. The package Dean delivered the other night still sits opened but unexplored in my room filled with sheet music that should excite me but instead feels like handcuffs.

"Oh my gosh, his compositions for violin are incredible! The way he blends classical pieces with modern elements..." She hugs her case to her chest and squeezes her eyes tight. "He's brilliant."

"Jules is..." I sigh, softly. "Someone who practices for hours every day." I grin at her. "Not a bad plan to follow if you have ambitious dreams."

She nods enthusiastically. "I will. I do already, I mean."

She didn't need to say it—I already know. The way she'd lost herself to the music, the sharp focus that narrowed her world down to the strings beneath her fingers. It was obvious. Emma doesn't just want this. She's working for it.

She snaps her case shut and slings it over her shoulder. "Well, I'm taking Mrs. Pierce up on the free ice cream!"

"See you Tuesday night?"

She grins as she opens the door. "I can't wait."

The light disappears, and the space turns back into quiet stillness—only mine and Dean's breaths echoing together.

I move back toward Giuseppe and loosen the bow. "Just how long do you plan to observe lessons?"

"Just how long do you plan to conduct them?" Dean steps toward me again. My pulse quickens. I haven't forgotten the moment Rachel interrupted earlier. I haven't thought about it, either. This man is like lightning against a dark sky. Electric, alive, and carrying a raw kind of power that feels impossible to ignore.

Dean stops walking a few steps in front of me and shoves his hands into his pockets. "Can't say I've had the opportunity to see a world-class performer in a private concert before." His lips twitch upward. "I'm impressed, Ms. Sinclair."

I wipe down the strings and fingerboard with a soft cloth and refuse to look up and meet his intense expression. "Was that a compliment? Careful, Dean. I think you're warming up to me."

His voice dips lower, the gravelly sound of it amplified in the room. "You don't make it easy to stay cold."

I lift my face. He's standing in a puddle of golden light, half of him in shadows which sculpt his features, cutting across his defined jaw and emphasizing his brow. I want to swallow hard. I want to stand up and finish whatever we started before Rachel and Emma arrived. I want—

The door opens again and we both jump. Alex's eyes flick between the two of us then she tightens her grip on her handbag. "Ready for lunch?"

"Yeah, of course." I leap up and ease Giuseppe back into his case, then latch it carefully. I need the moment to catch my breath. God, I swear Dean Markham is like discovering coffee —unexpected, slightly addicting, a little too strong, and suddenly I can't imagine going without it.

He nods and produces a fresh mint from somewhere. "Ladies."

Alex watches him go with an expression I can't quite read. When she turns back to me, there's a tightness around her eyes and she hasn't released her grip on the bag.

"Don't you need to work?" I ask, trying to shift the subject.

"With my sister in town, I can be flexible! How often do I get to see you?" She loops her arm through mine, but there's something protective in the gesture.

As we step outside together, I realize three essential truths that settle into my chest like a bad cold.

First, despite my attempts to carve out my own space here, I'm still pulling Alex off-rhythm. She's falling right back into the role of rearranging her world to care for me.

Second, I'm offering to mentor Emma while my own musical future sits disregarded in a package in my room and

Jules' emails remain unread. I'm more adrift career-wise than I realized, and that leaves a gnawing sense of dread aching in my stomach.

And third—the thought that causes me to miss a step on the way out and Alex to frown as she steadies me—this electric current between Dean and me is a problem. Because the last thing I need is something further throwing off my focus. And, more importantly, the last thing Alex needs is for me to complicate her world even more by falling for someone who holds power here.

Each step away from the studio feels like moving farther from something I shouldn't want but can't quite forget—a melody stuck in my head long after the song stopped playing.

Dean

Dawn spills over Magnolia Cove like honey, catching in the crimson maple leaves and glinting off brass door knockers that have weathered a century of coastal storms. I don't normally muse on the town's appearance, but lately everything golden reminds me of her eyes. The thought arrives unbidden, unwanted, yet persistent as the autumn wind carries the scent of the Whisk's cinnamon rolls down Main Street.

Monitoring yesterday's lessons between Missy and Emma rush through my thoughts and I grind my teeth.

Of course I knew she was a professional performer—I noted her credentials in that council application I shouldn't have approved—but watching her was something else entirely. I couldn't tear myself away from seeing how she immersed herself in the music, swaying like a flame in the wind, drawing out notes that hummed until they vibrated into my bones.

The magnetic pull between us grew stronger with each shared glance. I shouldn't have let it happen. Shouldn't have stepped so close in that whisper-quiet room, shouldn't have imagined closing the distance between us or brushing her hair away from the soft line of her neck.

But when she's all graceful curves and teasing smiles, when she's someone willing to look me in the eye, who seems to hold no secrets in her gaze and isn't afraid of what she might find in mine—it makes me forget every carefully constructed wall. It makes me long for things I gave up the day I chose the greater good over personal happiness, the magical community over my sister's love.

Main Street stretches before me, picture perfect with its cobblestone charm and meticulously maintained storefronts. Marcus' bookstore cat, Anne-With-An-E twines around books in A Novel Idea's window display. An old oak drips Spanish moss before it.

It's all small-town charm and carefully curated whimsy, the kind of place tourists photograph without ever truly seeing. They miss how magic pulses beneath every pristine awning and around each weathered brick.

Just like The Cove's residents miss the weight that comes with protecting it all. With being the one who stands between two worlds.

I trace the existing ward lines with practiced efficiency, reinforcing weak points where they've grown thin. Autumn always brings with it a treacherous dance between what humans call weather patterns and what we know as magical convergence. The wards, like everything else in Magnolia Cove, are tied to nature's rhythms—to lunar cycles, tide patterns, and the very breath of seasons changing.

And hurricane season tests every magical defense we have.

The ward pulses beneath my touch, responding to my magic and warning of instability. They're stretched thinner than usual, pulled taut between astronomical forces that even the council's oldest texts struggle to fully explain. One strong storm with our wards not reinforced could shred our protective veils like Spanish moss in a gale.

Another reason I can't afford distractions. Can't let

honey-warm eyes and musical laughter make me forget the weight of my responsibilities.

That's when I hear it. Music drifting across the morning stillness, rich and mournful. I know that sound. Already recognize the player.

I follow it to the festival grounds, where Missy sits in the exact center of the ward nexus, completely oblivious to the magic currents swirling around her. Her eyes are closed, head tilted as she draws her bow across Giuseppe's strings. The rising sun gilds her hair gold, and for a moment, she looks like she belongs here—part of the magic rather than separate from it.

The wards respond to her playing, rippling like water disturbed by stones. It's subtle, but I can feel their resonance shifting, adapting her music's rhythm. My own magic stirs in response, reaching toward her like a flower seeking light.

I shouldn't find it beautiful. Shouldn't want to watch how she sways with the music or find it irresistible to look away from the curves of her fingers.

Yesterday comes back to me without my consent. The way her lips looked in the gold-colored room. How she looked up at me, her long lashes framing her amber eyes. The energy that sizzled between us and everything that went unspoken.

But the magic within me isn't focused on Missy's playing or the way her hair slides down her shoulder and drapes across the bare skin of her collarbone.

It's fixed on the wards and whatever the hell they're doing. She's not breaking them, but she's making them behave strangely.

"The acoustics are better by the gazebo," I say, making her jump.

Her startled expression melts into that dangerous smile— the one that makes me forget all the reasons this is a terrible idea. The wards beneath my feet pulse a warning I'm choosing to ignore.

"Do you always lurk around watching people practice?" Morning mist curls around her ankles, drawn to her presence like magic seems to be. Like I'm determined to be, apparently, despite every hard-learned lesson screaming in protest.

"Only when they're trespassing in restricted areas." I slide my hands into my pockets. I shouldn't engage in this conversation, shouldn't let myself be pulled into her orbit. And yet here I stand, like a moth convinced this particular flame might not burn.

"Restricted?" She glances around the empty field. "It's just grass."

"Grass that's off limits. Besides,"—I speak over whatever she had parted her ruby lips to interject with—"are *you* always sitting around playing... Saint-Saëns?"

The composer's name emerges half-guess, half-memory. A fragment of my past when music and magic danced freely together, before duty drew sharp lines between what I wanted and what I had to become.

Her laugh spills across the morning air like sunlight through stained glass, warm and rich and somehow sacred. "Chopin, actually. *Nocturne in C-sharp Minor.*" She tilts her head, her eyes sparkling. "I have to say, I didn't expect the grumpy head of the council to know his classical composers."

The warmth in her voice beckons me like a siren's song, tempting me to share about my childhood music lessons. How my parents wanted me to play viola, but all I wanted to learn was rock music. How we compromised on the classical guitar. About Nell and I arguing over practice times, sheet music scattered across our family room while magic sparked between our fingers and glided down her flute's silvery body.

But those memories are better left buried. "There are a lot of things you don't know about me, Miss Sinclair."

"Missy," she corrects, rising from her makeshift seat with a grace that draws my eyes despite my best intentions. She gently wipes Giuseppe down and places him back in his case before looking back over her shoulder at me, her eyes filled with the clouds' reflections. "And me not knowing you is something we could change, you know?"

My heart hammers. There's a part of me that wants to cross the grass between us, to let duty and distance dissolve like morning mist. To discover if her skin carries the same warmth as her music, if her laugh tastes as sweet as it sounds.

I long to forget my role here, and Alex's disapproval, and Missy's magicless state, and a wedding invitation sitting in my office reminding me of similar bad choices in the past. And their cost.

Unfortunately, I can't forget those things. In the decade I've lived and worked here, they've become part of me. A vine wound around a tree until it imprinted on it.

"Or maybe not." Missy's voice sounds almost insecure, but she shrugs it off. "Maybe grumpy gnomes are unknowable."

I can't help the smile that pushes my lips up. That ridiculous label shouldn't draw me in deeper, and yet it does. Because in these teasing words, I hear something rare—someone who sees past the carefully constructed walls, past the stern authority, past the weight of magical responsibility. Everyone else in Magnolia Cove treats me like a living ward stone, necessary but cold, protective, and impersonal. But Missy... She looks at me and tries to see Dean.

Maybe that's why I hear myself ask, "Isn't it a bit early for Chopin, anyway?"

She traces a pattern on her cello case, her fingers moving like they're playing invisible strings. "I'm out here trying to remember why I fell in love with music in the first place."

There's a weight to her voice, a heaviness that pulls her shoulders and lips down.

"That surprises me." She lifts her face as I speak. "Alex lights up every time she talks about her talented little sister. About how music isn't just what you do, it's who you are. She talks about it so much everyone in town now claims to know you, even if they've never listened to a single classical composition."

The moment the words leave my mouth, I know they're wrong. Instead of grinning, her muscles tense, like bow strings pulled too taut, her smile flickering like a candle caught in the wind. I've seen that expression before—in mirrors, in memories, in moments when duty and desire wage their endless war. The look of someone drowning in others' expectations.

A beat of silence stretches between us, potent with unspoken truths. She's wearing a tan romper and pale blue cardigan and it's like she's fading into the sky and elements surrounding her. The word *angel* comes to my mind, then I immediately banish it.

I'm not a spiritual man. I trust magic I can touch, power I can trace through ward lines and protection spells. Looking at Missy, kissed by morning light, I wonder if touching her might make me believe in something more than magic. Something dangerous. Something real. My fingers flex in my pockets, brushing the familiar edge of the medallion.

"Jules fits perfectly in all of it," she says suddenly, her voice as soft as the sun's morning rays. "The touring, the spotlight, the constant motion. It's like he was born for it." She wraps her arms around her cello case, like it's a shield she can hold against herself. "Can I tell you something? Something that stays between us?"

Her eyes have gone soft and large, seeking. I shouldn't encourage confidence. Shouldn't let her trust me. And yet I find myself saying, "Of course."

"I'm terrified of disappointing Alex." The words leave her like something she's coughing up, raspy and painful. "She gave up everything for my dream. But what if it was never really my dream at all?"

I take a step forward. Stop. I was about to reach out for her, touch her. Before I can remember all the reasons I shouldn't. I curl my fingers into fists, then let them fall. "Alex loves you." The words feel inadequate, as obvious as the wards pulsing beneath our feet. Everyone on the island knows the depth of Alex Sinclair's devotion to her sister.

"What does love mean, though?"

She's looking up at me, sunlight brushing along her eyelashes and kissing her cheeks in ways I can't. There's a dusting of freckles across her nose like stars. The wards dance beneath me. I should shift my attention to them, to the magic they're drawing off me. But I can't look away from this woman standing before me.

Her question hangs in the morning quiet, dangerous as exposed magic. What does love mean? To sacrifice everything like Alex did for her? To walk away like I did for Nell? To stand here now, fighting the magnetic pull of honey-gold eyes while duty whispers its constant cautions?

"Love means..." My voice emerges rough, like I've forgotten how to shape words that matter. "I think it means seeing someone as they truly are and loving them exactly for that. And maybe it means doing what's best for them, even when it's difficult for you. And I think your sister has that for you, Missy."

Her name on my lips feels like casting a spell—something powerful and precise and impossible to take back. Magic thrums around us, aching into my bones. I should have a headache from it, but I only feel an intense sense of clarity. The rising sun has turned her eyes to amber and her breath catches at my words, her gasp the only sound I can hear.

Dangerous, this honesty. More dangerous still, how much I want to keep offering it.

Her fingers ghost across Giuseppe's case. "And what about you, Dean? Who sees you exactly as you are?"

The question strikes like lightning bypassing carefully constructed shields. In her gaze, I see past and present collide —the weight of Nell's wedding invitation, the pressure of council expectations, the constant vigilance required of one of Magnolia Cove's protectors.

And beneath it all, a treacherous whisper that maybe, just maybe, I've met someone who finally could see me for who I am, regardless.

She breaks the spell first, offering a smile that carries too many meanings to decipher. "Well, I suppose I should try the gazebo then. Don't want to get a reprimand from the grumpy gnome council." She smirks and shifts her cello case on her shoulder. "I'll see you Tuesday, right?"

"Right," I whisper, unable to form more words. She smiles anyway, and I feel caught under an enchantment, unable to move or breathe.

She turns, Giuseppe's case swaying gently as she steps away. The sun has risen more during our conversation and it bathes her in gold. She pauses at the field's edge and glances back over her shoulder. For a moment, she's silhouetted against the dawn—half tangible, half dream.

Then she's gone, leaving only the echo of her presence in the air. In the quiet that follows, I notice something else. The wards beneath my feet have settled, their usual chaotic hurricane of magical energy smoothed to gentle waves. Like a storm suddenly calmed, like magic finding its natural rhythm.

I crouch down and press a palm against the ground. The power pulses steadily into my fingertips, matching the rhythm of my heartbeat. While I'd spoken with Missy, the magic had pulled at me—not fought, not strained, but reached. Reached for me but also her, like I'd forced myself not to do.

The wards ripple beneath my touch, strong as heartwood. These are the same volatile boundaries I'd come to reinforce, the same weakened protections that should have taken hours of careful work to stabilize. Now they hum with renewed vitality, as if...

No. That's impossible.

I trace my fingers down the grass where magic courses, searching for any sign of manipulation or external influence. But there's only the pure, steady thrum of magic finding its natural rhythm. Like a symphony settling into its perfect harmony and—

The thought stops me cold.

She's a normal human. Magicless. Yet something about her presence seems to calm the very forces I've spent years learning to control. The same forces that are at their crankiest in the autumn during storm season.

I rise slowly. Above, the sky has cleared to a perfect cerulean. The morning mist has burned away completely, leaving only the ghostly impression of the lingering scent of vanilla and rosin in its wake.

I'd planned to spend the entire morning reinforcing the wards. Now they're steady, not needing my intervention.

My fingers find the medallion in my pocket again. Some mysteries require too much thinking before breakfast.

But as I turn back toward town, I can't help but wonder what other impossible things Missy Sinclair might be capable of awakening in Magnolia Cove. In its magic.

In me.

Dean

Notes scattered across my desk paint a fragmented picture of impossibility. Yellowed pages from my father's journals, official council records dating back centuries, even controversial texts I've pulled from Magnolia Cove's restricted archives. None of them explain what I witnessed Missy do to the ward lines though. What I keep witnessing.

My fingers trace the edge of another useless page while an autumn gale rattles the cottage windows. I have only the single lamp on, the glow casting long shadows past a well-worn leather chair and my stacked bookshelves to the guitar sitting quietly against the wall, waiting. I let my eyes linger on it for a moment before pushing the thought aside. There's no time for distractions today.

Words blur together, meaningless academic observations about humans with magical sensitivity. It's primarily focused on how to obscure the perception of magic, how to perform memory magic when necessary to erase things that shouldn't have been seen, and what to do when minds resist magical influence.

Not a single damn word written about music that calms

wards, or about someone's magic being influenced by a human's presence, or honey-warm eyes that melt the firmest defenses. I've even skimmed my sister's recently published research—she's one of the foremost researchers of living magical theory at Calthorne, the top magical university in our country. If anyone would know of such discoveries, it's her. Reading her work feels like pressing against a door she's closed, and the sting is knowing she continues to shape the field we once shared, while I stand on the outside by choice.

I rub my temples, a low hum of frustration rising in my chest.

The box sitting on the kitchen counter taunts me with its cheerful orange ribbon and familiar handwriting. Mom always loved autumn. She probably has pumpkins stacked on her porch steps and a wreath of dried leaves hanging on the door.

I've avoided the package all morning, like ignoring it might make it disappear. Might make the thing deep inside stop tugging at me. As if distance has ever made anything easier.

I rise and stretch then cross toward the box. Better to get it over with. At least Mom and Dad aren't visiting this month. Her tears—always about how she wishes things could be fixed—are something I don't have the fortitude for, even on my most focused days.

I untie the ribbon, letting it drop against the butcher block countertop. A tin sits on top and even before I get the lid fully off, the scent hits. Cinnamon—rich and slightly woody—blended with ginger's bite and a faint touch of nutmeg, all wrapped together in sugar's sweetness.

Mom's autumn spice cookies.

Magic shimmers over them, preserving them. But Mom's love preserves more. A memory comes to me unbidden.

Dean is taking the last cookie! Nell is maybe seven standing with fists propped on her hips.

She's eaten more than me! I'm indignant. Ten and knowing I can do no wrong. Arrogant enough to truly believe that.

Mom, so much younger and less worried, only smiles and swipes her hand, slicing the cookie perfectly down the middle. *There's plenty to share. And we'll make more later.*

I put the lid back on the cookie tin and move it aside. Beneath, there's a sweater, black as night and just as soft. Mom's knitted protection charms into every stitch and they hum, as comforting as a whispered prayer. Some mothers send care packages. Mine sends armor disguised as comfort in a color she doesn't prefer seeing on me, but knows it's all I'll wear.

The letter is last, of course. Mom's elegant script flows across the page, filled with ordinary words—book club opinions, council gossip, wedding preparations. No mention of my absence. No guilt. Just the weight of everything left unsaid pressed between carefully chosen phrases.

The roses for the ceremony are coming along beautifully, though I sometimes wish we had your preservation abilities. Your father always said you handled temperamental magic with such ease.

I fold the letter without reading farther. I can only take so much of this—the gentle pressure, the expectations wrapped in kindness.

My sister's face rises unbidden to my mind, her expression the last time I saw her—nose flaring, lips thin, tears spilling from unblinking eyes to streak down reddened cheeks.

I can't undo what happened, can't make things right. The clock chimes two, its sound echoing through my too-empty house. Time for Emma's lesson. Time to watch Missy coax impossible things from ordinary moments. To stand alert for whatever she's doing to make the magic... unpredictable. To pretend like that's what draws me in, not the curve of her lips or the tenor of her laughter.

I leave the cookie tin unopened and step out, not bothering to lock the door. Even if someone dared to break into my house, the wards I've set in place would keep them out. Except, perhaps, for Missy.

That thought hangs on me as I begin the walk beneath a cloud-filled sky.

* * *

Rachel's studio seems alive with music, even in its silence, as warm light dances along the curves of instruments and glints off polished brass fixtures. Today it holds something else—a current in the air that has nothing to do with the wards I maintain and everything to do with the way Missy's fingers dance across Giuseppe's strings.

I lean against the wall, keeping my lips pressed together, my gaze distant and bored even as I fight the urge to close my eyes and let her music wash over me. Emma follows Missy's lead, her own playing growing more confident with each measure. The magic within the young witch rises and falls like tides against the shore—volatile but not dangerous. Not yet.

Rachel makes another obscene slurping sound with her iced coffee beside me. I shoot her a glare that would send most residents scurrying. She just grins and rattles her ice. She's always been impertinent, and given her family's long-standing roots in Magnolia Cove, I suppose she's earned the right.

"Emma's pretty good, huh?" she whispers.

"Mhmm." Her musical abilities are excellent. Her magical ones even more so. But I'm not getting caught in Rachel's web of probing questions.

She takes another long, obnoxious slurp. "You know,"—she whispers, as though pretending to preserve the quiet actually matters to her—"glowering at everyone isn't actually required by the council bylaws last time I checked."

"And when was that?"

She grins like a shark around her straw. "Wouldn't you like to know?"

A music teacher makes one viral video and saves a small music program and she thinks she's queen of Magnolia Cove now. The way Rachel always acts like she has the inside track on everything drives me crazy. But the worst part is that she's often right and if she isn't, she makes her goals happen, anyway.

"I'm focusing on my job," I say. "Not everyone gets distracted by performances."

She leans back against the wall then crosses her ankles. "Oh, I don't know. Seems like you've been a bit distracted to me."

The sheer audacity. Maybe my guard has come down too much if a Cove resident feels bold enough to speak to her Head Warlock this way. I'm about to say something to that effect when Missy looks up from where she sits in a pool of soft gray light and smiles like sunshine—eyes crinkling at the corners, joy radiating from every curve. I can almost hear her voice in my head, teasing me about grumpy gnomes.

My lips betray me, curving up without permission. One small crack in carefully constructed walls, and somehow she floods right through.

Missy turns her attention back to Emma. They begin another song, and I pull a breath mint loose then pop it into my mouth.

Rachel's voice drops to a true whisper, so quiet even I can barely hear it standing next to her. "Alex is pretty protective of her little sister."

I swallow. "I know."

I do. The last person Rachel needs to convince me that my growing feelings for Missy are a bad idea is me. I'm trying to think of a response. Maybe a blatant lie. *There's nothing there to worry about.* Or a full truth. *It's none of your business.* Before I can respond, words die in my throat.

The magic in the room has... shifted. No—transformed. The usual chaos of Emma's powers, the wild energy that makes her such a challenging student, such a potentially powerful witch if she ever learns to control it, has suddenly... settled.

Rachel and I both turn toward the music. Missy stands behind Emma, her hands resting lightly on the girl's shoulders as she plays. The piece—something by Tchaikovsky—fills the space with impossible richness, as if an entire orchestra plays through Emma's violin. But it's not just the music that's extraordinary.

Emma's magic has found its rhythm, flowing smooth and controlled as spring water. No surges, no sparks, just pure harmonious power guided by Missy's presence. A presence that should have no effect on magic at all.

Rachel's iced coffee hangs forgotten halfway to her mouth. Even I can't maintain my carefully neutral expression. In all my years of studying magic, all my research into humans with unusual sensitivity, I've seen nothing like this.

The piece ends. Missy breaks into applause and jumps onto her toes as if she needs to cheer from the highest position she can attain. And then she looks at me.

Her eyes glisten and search. Always searching. Something inside me shifts like tectonic plates realigning. The magic in my blood hums in response, growls with desires I've spent years suppressing. It coils tight, a deep primal urge that's thrumming with questions I'm not ready to answer.

I shouldn't want this. Shouldn't want her. But in this moment, even with Rachel watching, with the evidence of impossible things singing between us all, I can't remember why.

* * *

Midnight finds me at my desk, one of Mom's cookies forgotten beside a stack of grimoires. A single bite taken and the spices still linger on my tongue like memories of simpler days. The ward-locked journal lies open before me, its pages filling with observations that read more like confessions.

Subject demonstrates unprecedented harmonization with magical frequencies...

I pause, press the nib of my pen against the paper until ink bleeds through. Clinical language can't capture the way Missy's presence transforms magic itself. How does one document something that defies documentation? Something that feels less like observation and more like witness to a miracle?

When in proximity to the subject, ward stability increases by approximately...

My writing stops again. Nothing about her effect on magic can be measured in percentages and parameters. Nothing about her effect on me fits in these careful notes.

The truth hovers between the lines I can't bring myself to write: that maybe it's not just her presence affecting the wards. Maybe it's the way my magic reaches for her like the tide drawn by the moon. The way power surges beneath my skin when she smiles. How everything feels more alive, more possible, when she's near.

But that's not something I can commit to paper. Not something I can let myself examine too closely. Because if my attraction to her influences the wards' response...

I drop the pen. There's no point in maintaining this pretense of academic observation. These notes are as false as Magnolia Cove's non-magical facade we craft for visitors.

Who sees you exactly as you are?

Missy's words from before echo in my head, golden as the

dawn light that cascaded over her. The question lingers along-side the clove and cinnamon spices, demanding an answer I'm not ready to give.

The cookie crumbles beneath my fingers as I reach for it blindly. Outside, waves crash against the shore in a rhythm that reminds me of her playing. Of Emma's magic finding its harmony under her touch. Of something that shouldn't be possible becoming beautifully, terrifyingly real.

My father's journals lie scattered across the desk, their margins filled with his precise handwriting. I used to find comfort in his methodical approach to magical theory. Now his certainties feel like accusations. *Magic follows rules, Dean. Understanding those rules is the key to controlling them.*

But what if that isn't true?

Missy breaks every rule simply by existing. Seeing past wards is rare for humans, but not unheard of. Her sister has the same issue. Calming magic, though? Strengthening the wards? Making me feel...

My fingers crush together, and the cookie crumbles over my desk. I wipe the mess away. Pick the pen back up.

Further observation required to determine the extent of the subject's influence on magical energy patterns.

Maybe this is what finding faith feels like—this terrifying certainty that something exists beyond explanation. Beyond control. Beyond something a person can tame, understand, or capture in neatly organized notes.

I close the journal, its wards humming softly in the dark-ness. Tomorrow I'll go back to being the council's perfect protector, the son who stays away to ensure his sister's happi-ness, the warlock who puts duty before desire.

But tonight, in the quiet hours between midnight and dawn, I let myself remember the way my magic danced when Missy smiled. How her music made impossible things feel inevitable. The weight of her in my arms and how her laughter echoed into me.

Maybe that's the most dangerous magic of all.

Missy

A clatter of laughter and conversations fill the town square and light spills across the space like honey dripping from a spoon, catching on the half-constructed leaf arch that looks more like a botanical disaster than the elegant entrance Grammie Rae seems to have envisioned.

It took precisely thirty seconds of me meeting the woman before she insisted I call her Grammie. She also told me she was Emma's actual grandmother and listed off all the town's most eligible bachelors.

She stands beneath the arch now, silver curls tucked beneath a ball cap, wrinkled hands fisted on her hips over a pair of practical overalls. "Tom, honey, those mums need to be at least six inches to the left. No, your other left." She throws her hands in the air. "This is why I told the council we needed a professional."

Tom shoves the flowers a third direction and laughs. "Last time I'll spend my day off volunteering."

"Good." Grammie Rae weaves more leaves into the arch. "Maybe the council will actually become useful and hire people who know what they're doing."

"I heard that," Dean calls from where he's helping arrange pumpkins by the gazebo. His all-black ensemble makes him look like a crow among autumn leaves, but somehow he pulls it off. Not that I'm noticing.

Rachel appears beside me, two steaming cups in hand. "Your sister's cinnamon lattes are dangerous," she says, passing one over. The rich scent fills the air between us as the heat warms my hands. Rachel laughs before taking a drink. "I've had three already, and it's not even noon."

"Alex's specialty is making things addictive. She didn't get a cookbook deal for nothing." I take a sip, the creamy richness blending seamlessly with the nutty flavor of espresso. I try not to think about how many things in Magnolia Cove fall into the *addictive* category. Like the way certain council members look when they're concentrating on perfectly spacing gourds.

"Speaking of addictive," Rachel says like she's read my mind. I can't help the heat that flushes my cheeks. "Emma's been different since you've started teaching her. There's something about the way she plays now..." She trails off, watching Emma twirl in her burnt-orange dress and laughing with other teens from the music program. "I can't explain it in words really, but thank you."

She keeps dancing around whatever she really wants to say, keeps exchanging strange looks with Dean although they seem to barely tolerate each other. There's some mystery happening here. When I shared that with Alex last night, she'd become flighty, tossing her wedding magazine to the side and jumping up to 'do the dishes' despite me having already washed them earlier.

I try to think of a careful question I could ask that might unravel whatever Magnolia Cove hides. There's a part of me that wonders if Alex really joined a cult. Part of me wonders if I want to join it as well.

Just as I'm about to speak, Mrs. Delehay's Pomeranian

makes a break for freedom, then gets tangled in the raffia streamers Tom's trying to hang. The chaos that follows prompts Grammie Rae to throw her hands in the air, dramatically calling for divine intervention.

Iris, the florist, giggles and covers her laugh with her fingers. "At least the dog has good taste. Those streamers are a crime against autumn."

Tom untangles himself then freezes and gapes at her. "You act like I chose the material. I'd like to see you do better."

"That's what she's been trying to explain for twenty minutes," Grammie Rae says with a wink that makes Iris laugh harder. Tom sticks his tongue out at her, and without missing a beat, Iris does the same, her grin wide as she mimics him. They burst into laughter together.

I hide my smile in my coffee cup. There's something about this town that makes everything feel like a story waiting to happen. Even now, watching Emma with her friends, I can see her future unfolding like sheet music—full of possibility and promise.

A warm breeze carries the scent of fresh baked goods from Main Street and mingles with the sweetness of Iris' chrysanthemums. A group of children toss a baseball around and wave at Tom. Their laughter rings under the cloudy sky as a wind picks up fallen, brown magnolia and maple leaves, tumbling them across the clearing. My fingers itch to pick up Giuseppe, to capture this moment in music.

Not with the desire to write something that would match the polished pieces Jules keeps sending, but something real. Something that tastes like cinnamon and feels like belonging.

Speaking of Jules... My useless phone is like a weight in my pocket. It's filled with emails—messages from Jules asking for updates and complaining about me gallivanting off to a small town with no cell service, just like he'd expected. Then there are the messages from our tour manager, fans reaching out, interview requests piling up. And I've answered none of them.

My stomach twists. Later. I swear to myself I'll deal with it later.

"All right everyone!" Rachel claps her hands. "Let's run through the music once before lunch."

The kids file into chairs or position themselves behind music stands, some adjusting their instruments, others fumbling with their sheet music.

Emma takes her spot for the violin solo, tucking the instrument under her chin. The opening floats out perfectly, her bow gliding effortlessly. The sound is clear and resonant, a stark contrast to the hesitant playing and occasional jarring notes from other students. But then—a fumble. Emma's bow skids across the strings and the wind picks up, sending sheet music scattering and flowers tumbling. Something shifts in the air, like pressure building before a storm.

I take a step toward Emma, but Dean's already there, crouching beside her chair. His voice carries just enough for me to catch the words.

"Overwhelmed?"

She bats back tears and bows her head. "I'm not going to be able to do this. Play at the Hoopla, much less go to Juilliard. I'll never get it."

I expect Dean's usual stern council member response. Instead, his voice softens into something that makes my heart do complicated things in my chest.

"Someone once gave me advice about what the difference between a good musician and a great one is."

She sniffles and looks up. "What's that?"

"A good musician practices until they get it right. Great ones practice until they can't get it wrong. That's true for... other things as well. At least, that's what an annoying perfectionist of a sister used to tell me."

Emma's laugh comes out watery but real. "You have a sister?"

"Once upon a time." Something flickers across his face and I remember the black-and-white print in his office, pointed where only visitors can see it, nowhere within his own line of sight. Dean couldn't have been more than eight in the picture. His younger sister, with hair just as dark as his, rests her head on his shoulder, her toothless grin wide and full of mischief. "My sister was a lot like you—too much talent to contain sometimes."

The tenderness in his voice hits me like a physical thing. I've seen Dean frustrated, amused, even almost playful on rare occasions. But this—this unguarded moment—feels more intimate than any of our almost-kisses.

Which is exactly why I need to stop watching him like he's a puzzle I want to solve. Stop noticing how his broad shoulders fill out his jacket, how the curve of his jaw catches the light just so, or how his eyes darken when he's deep in thought.

I have a career to save, an album to finish, a life waiting in cities with names that taste like ambition. I don't have time to join a cult, charming or otherwise. Anyway, I'll leave Magnolia Cove in a few months.

And maybe most importantly, I don't need to complicate Alex's life here. She's happy and at ease. Her sister dating the most *difficult* guy in town would only stir up things. I can't risk...

Emma's violin sings out again, steady and sure this time. The wind settles. Tom and Iris throw leaves at each other and laugh. Then Tom ducks behind hay bales to avoid the next round.

Dean stands and our eyes meet. The look he gives me feels like recognition, like seeing and being seen, like...

No. Absolutely not.

I turn away first and focus on Grammie Rae who's now muttering something about how 'herding cats would be easier than organizing this festival' and how she's 'too blessed to be stressed, but current circumstances are making me reconsider that.'

I'm just caught up in the romance of a small-town life, in the way everything here feels touched by some kind of everyday magic.

But I know better than anyone—magic isn't real, and some songs are meant to stay unfinished.

"Dessert at Sinclair's?" Rachel appears at my elbow, her eyes bright. "Alex is testing some new fall recipes and the whole gang's coming. We're extremely qualified and helpful when it comes to taste-testing. It's basically our favorite activity."

The weight of my phone tugs against me again. Jules' last email burns like an accusation against my hip. *This is exactly what I expected to happen. When you're done falling off the face of the earth, could you message me back?*

The compositions for our albums still sit untouched in my room, his careful notations awaiting my response. His career partially rides on this collaboration, on the trust he placed in me as his partner.

I should say no to Rachel. Should head home and lose myself to the complex harmonies we've been building together for months. Should be the responsible artist he needs.

Dean looks up from where he's still speaking with Emma as she packs up her violin. Something in his gaze makes my breath catch—like he sees past all my carefully constructed walls to the messy truth beneath. To the part that's tired of being perfect, that wants to choose joy over obligation just once.

I smile at Rachel and shrug, as if my heart isn't racing, as if this isn't another minor act of rebellion against the life I'm supposed to want. "Sure, that sounds great."

The compositions can wait another day. After all, some of the best music comes from the space between the notes—the moments that allow for a breath.

Jules would hate that kind of thinking. But watching Dean help Emma to her feet, seeing the way his stern expression softens when she hugs him impulsively, I'm starting to wonder if that's exactly why I need to think it.

Dean

Weather, like magic, can shift without warning.

A few hours ago, the sun warmed pumpkins on hay bales and kids licked cider popsicles in the park. Now lightning splits the sky, illuminating the chaos below. Palm fronds and Spanish moss whip through the air, while thunder growls warnings across Magnolia Cove's darkened streets. I raise my voice above the storm's fury.

"Reinforce the residential wards first. Standard emergency protocols."

Gerald nods, rainwater streaming from his hood. "There's rotation in those clouds. We could be looking at a tornado."

"Then we need the wards stronger than ever." I scan the gathering darkness, marking each council member's position. "Take your usual sections. I'll handle the nexus points."

"Grammie Rae was out earlier," Sarah calls over a rising gust. "Trying to save the Hoopla decorations."

Of course she was. I press fingers to my temples, fighting the urge to grind my teeth. Keeping magical beings alive is like trying to wrangle toddlers with boundless curiosity but no sense of self-preservation. "Get everyone secured in their homes. We'll need to channel most of the wards' magic into protecting residential areas tonight. We'll deal with cleanup tomorrow."

"But the Hoopla—"

"Has survived sixty-three years of storms." I cut off Cordelia's protest. "And we still have three weeks until it's time. The wards are secure there. Even if we need to replace a few pumpkins, it'll survive. This won't be the year we miss."

The group scatters into the tempest, leaving me to tackle the most complex ward lines. They pulse beneath the island's surface like arteries of pure magic. And lately, they seem to resonate with a certain cellist's music.

I shove that thought aside and push through the whipping winds. Mom's protection sweater helps, the magic she knitted into each stitch humming against my skin. But something feels... off. The wards aren't just straining against the storm. They're fluctuating, rippling in a pattern I've never felt before.

Following the disturbance takes me down debris-littered paths toward the music performance hall. Tree branches scrape against my jacket, leaving scratches despite the protective magic. But beneath the storm's rage, I hear it—cello music, as rich and haunting as a midnight confession.

I wrench the door open against the wind. It pulls like it's going to yank my shoulder out of its socket. Missy sits bathed in silver moonlight, hair braided over one shoulder, completely lost in whatever she's playing. Her head snaps up at my entrance. "Dean?"

I haul the door closed behind me with a full-body yank. The lock clicks into place—and just like that, the storm's fury is muffled to a dull, distant roar. The sudden quiet is jarring.

"What are you doing out here in this storm?" The words come out harsher than intended, rough and crazed with a fear I'm not ready to examine.

She looks to the windows then color floods her cheeks.

"I'm sorry. I didn't realize how bad it had gotten. When I can't sleep, I play and I didn't want to wake Alex and Ethan. I didn't realize..." She trails off, her elegant fingers sliding down Giuseppe's strings.

"You could get hurt." The raw honesty in my voice has me taking a step back. Missy raises her face at that and her expression softens into something unreadable. There's a vulnerability in her gaze, a quiet understanding that hits me harder than I expect. The tension between us lingers, thick and charged, but she doesn't say a word.

A violent gust rattles the windows. Magic crackles through the air like static and the wards vibrate as they strain against nature's fury. I wince. "Power's flickering. I should check it."

That's when she speaks, and her voice comes out haunted, echoing against the high ceilings. "There's no power in here right now, Dean."

I freeze, my hand caught on the doorknob. She's right—the studio lies in darkness save for the storm-wracked moonlight spilling through the windows. A rookie mistake born of exhaustion and distraction.

Her eyes find mine, questions glistening across them. "That's not what you really do here. Check power, babysit musical teens, fill out forms? That's not your actual job, is it?"

Thunder punctuates the loaded silence between us. For once, I answer with truth instead of deflection. "No, it isn't." My voice roughens. "Let me check something. I'll be back in a few minutes."

Outside, I pour everything I have into reinforcing the wards, ones that stretch halfway across the island. Wind batters me as I brace against it. I can feel the pull of the magic, a deep, steady hum beneath the surface of everything. Each breath is a steady push as I layer the wards one by one, like building a wall brick by brick. The magic resists at first, pulling back and falling into step with the storm's erratic rhythm. But I force it, bending it to my will, snapping it into place and tightening the edges with brutal precision.

By the time I stagger back inside, the world spins at the edges of my vision.

Missy rises, her brow furrowed. "Are you okay?"

"I'm fine," I say, but I stumble a step.

"Sit down before you fall. Can I get you anything?"

I drop into a chair with a groan, nearly toppling it. "Play for me?"

She blinks and looks like she's about to protest, words hovering on her lips. Then her gaze softens and instead of arguing she moves toward her cello, finds her seat, and plays.

The first notes hum into the space, filling the emptiness and flooding my senses. I close my eyes and absorb it. The music, but also the way my magic calms beneath it, replenishes, finds a rhythm in time to hers.

I shouldn't want to understand this connection. Shouldn't let myself believe in whatever this is, or long for more.

But as the song swells around me, soothing the edges of my frayed thoughts and easing my physical exhaustion, it's hard not to. Each note she plays pulls at something deep inside me, a thread I didn't even know was there, unraveling with every breath.

"That's beautiful," I whisper when the final note fades. "What was it?"

"Fauré. *Elegie.*"

"I understand now why people pay hundreds of dollars to come see one of your shows."

"Been looking up my ticket prices, have you?" The smile in her voice causes me to open my eyes. Apparently tonight I'm wide open, letting everything slip without a filter. What the hell am I doing? I'm not supposed to be this... vulnerable. With anyone. Especially with her. But the way she looks at me, the way her music wraps around everything inside me, it's hard to keep that distance.

"Maybe I've considered coming to a show." The admission costs nothing now, here in the storm-dark quiet. I realize it's true. I'd like to see her dressed in some sparkling outfit that costs my weekly salary. See her gleaming beneath stage lights, pouring her talent out for people who rise and clap like thunder for her. I imagine the way she might stand there, confident and alive in the spotlight, and it feels like a lifetime away from this intimate moment between us.

"You play like it's magic," I whisper the words, barely audible, because I shouldn't say them.

I shouldn't—there's no way to describe what I'm feeling, what I'm seeing. But it's the truth. What she's doing now, here, in an ivory blouse under moonlight playing something that sounds like heaven itself opened up, could hardly seem more magical than any performance in front of an audience. Maybe she's an angel. Maybe I'm foolish enough to start believing in something after meeting her. Or maybe tonight's work has just sapped me more than I thought.

She turns her bow around in her hand then bats her eyes furiously but a tear slips free, anyway.

"I don't even know why I'm telling you this." She whispers too, like we're exchanging secrets. "But I haven't finished the album I'm supposed to be doing with Jules. I can't even look at the compositions. I just..." She falters, her fingers trembling. "Sometimes I think I've forgotten how to play for myself."

I sit higher in my chair. "*That* didn't sound like someone who's forgotten how to play."

She rests her chin against Giuseppe's shoulder. "That was just me playing for me," she says softly. "Not the shows, the lights, the applause. All that noise. Jules loves all of that—feeds off it, really. But maybe I don't." She runs her fingers along the cello's neck. "Maybe I've spent too long chasing what others want to hear, and I've forgotten what it feels like to just play because I *need* to."

"And now? Here?"

I need her to say it. For some reason, I long to hear her admit that Magnolia Cove is different, that it's changing something in her, that she wants to be here. That, maybe, someone as talented and beautiful and worldly as her might want somewhere—someone—who isn't part of the noise and the frenzy.

Thunder rumbles as she looks up. "I don't know what it is about this place," she whispers, "but... I've never felt like I can breathe the way I do here. Like there's space for me.... Just me. Not the performer. Not Margaret Sinclair. Just plain old Missy."

Her words hang in the air, and for a moment, everything feels impossibly still. Even the storm outside seems to take a breath to hold space for it. Like the weight of her confession has shifted something—like the magic here *wants* her, just as much as I do, if not more.

I swallow and don't break eye contact with her. "I'm honored to witness that."

She takes in a breath that feels like a promise. The storm kicks back up, leaves and sticks clattering against the windows. The world outside is chaotic, but in this room, it feels like time has slowed, like we're suspended in a space that belongs only to us.

I stand testing my strength. "I should get you and the cranky Italian home before your sister discovers you both missing and starts to worry."

"One grumpy soul looking out for another?" she teases, her following laugh sparkling in the darkness.

I smile. I don't even fight it. "It's a talent, I suppose."

She gently puts Giuseppe away, her fingers trailing the

wood reverently before tucking him into his case. "How do you know so much about classical music? Big orchestra buff?"

"I guess you could say that." Wind roars, causing the door to groan and Missy rushes to click the case's latches. I shift on my feet, restless and eager to get her somewhere safe. "As a teenager I played classical guitar. A lot. It was... an escape for me, I guess." I hesitate for a moment, then admit, "I still do, but only by myself."

She rises to her feet and sets Giuseppe's case against the wall, her eyes softening as she regards me. After a beat, she speaks, her voice quieter now. "I'd love to hear that one day."

"Maybe," I whisper, like the word is more fragile than I want to admit. I pull off my jacket then Mom's protection sweater. Missy's watching me in a way that has caused her expression to change. Her eyes have darkened, and she lifts them back up from where they'd lingered a moment too long, observing the slip of skin my ridden-up shirt exposed.

"Here," I say, my voice thick and filled with too much emotion. And completely out of my control for the moment. "You'll need this for the storm."

"What about you?"

"I've lived on this island for nearly a decade. I can handle a bit of rain."

Her breathing is heavy enough to cut through the wind's roar. The air seems to pulse with the unspoken. "Okay," she whispers as she accepts it, our fingers brushing.

She attempts to turn the sweater inside-out, but it gets tangled in her hand, the fabric pulling awkwardly. Her brow furrows, and she bites down on her lower lip.

"Let me help," I say.

She nods, and I step closer and accept the sweater then gently untangle it. As I pull it over her head, then down her shoulders, my fingers graze the curve of her hips, the touch electric, sending a rush of warmth through me.

I don't want to move my hands away. I want to curl them tighter, pull her closer to me. "Is this okay?"

She swallows then nods as she looks up at me. So close she smells like vanilla mixed with something else—something sweet and familiar with the faint hint of wood polish and strings, like her cello. It's intoxicating.

She raises her hands then rests them against my stomach, her fingers curling around my ribs. The touch is soft, but the way her fingers settle against me feels like an anchor, rooting me to the spot.

My heart pounds so hard it's drowning out my thoughts. Which is good. I don't want responsible, think-through-every-thing Dean at this moment. I want to breathe in her sweetness and feel the softness of her body beneath my hands and lean closer to her and—

"And this?" I barely whisper against her lips. "Is this okay?"

Her eyes flutter closed, and she leans in so that our noses touch. "More than okay."

With that, she pulls me in, closing the gap between us. Her lips meet mine with a gentle urgency, like she's hungered for this moment as much as I have. The kiss begins soft, but quickly deepens. She presses in closer, all softness and warmth in my arms. Her fingers find their way to my hair and grip. I groan into her mouth then slide a thumb down the column of her throat and press a kiss there and—

A deafening boom of thunder cracks through the room, making the walls shake. I pull back, force my hands to return to my side. "Let's get you home."

Missy nods once then grabs Giuseppe's case. I accept it and, when she's preoccupied for a moment, ward it with a water-repellent charm. The last thing I need is for her precious cello to get damaged in the downpour.

I wrench the door open again, and we battle the storm

together. I spend the entire walk warding her, keeping the worst of the storm at bay with subtle shifting spells—shielding us from the heaviest rain, steering the wind away, but it's exhausting. My energy is already stretched from the magic I've used today, and every extra bit pulls something from me, leaving me increasingly drained with each step.

At Ethan and Alex's door, she rises on her tiptoes and presses a soft kiss to my lips. "Good night, Dean."

"Good night, Missy."

In that one gesture, all the exhaustion and worry from the night feels worth it. I wait until she's safely inside, wrapped in layers of magical protection before turning toward my cottage. Soaked and trembling with exhaustion, I wearily pull my jacket off. I can't sleep until the storm passes. Until Magnolia Cove is once again safe.

I run my fingers across my lips, tracing the spot where hers had just touched.

Some storms change everything. Some magic defies explanation.

And some risks are worth taking.

Dean

Storm debris litters the festival grounds—broken branches, rain-soaked Spanish moss, and the occasional hay bale, left out in the open after its protection ward failed to hold, now drenched and flattened by the storm. I clutch an Americano from the Whisk against my chest as I trace the ward lines. Most parts held up. Others need reinforcement. Oddly, my magic feels settled this morning, despite the exhaustion weighing me down and caffeine being the only thing keeping me upright.

The damage could have been worse. Much worse, if not for...

I push away thoughts of moonlit music and vanilla-scented kisses. Force myself to focus on the task at hand. Grammie Rae's voice cuts across the field from where she's directing the cleanup crew with her particular blend of iron will wrapped in a grandmotherly Southern accent.

"Thomas Andrew Bryson, that is not where those pumpkins go. I know your grandmother taught you better than that."

Tom, arms full with a storm-dampened oversized

pumpkin that's soaked his flannel, shoots me a pleading look. "A little help here?"

I take a slow sip of coffee, grateful it's bitter enough to match my mood. "I distinctly recall suggesting we wait a few weeks to decorate."

"Oh, hush." Grammie Rae waves off my pragmatism with weathered hands. "The magic likes pretty things. Makes it feel appreciated."

I glance at Tom, raising an eyebrow and offering a look that probably conveys: *Sorry I have nothing to offer.* He groans but dumps the pumpkin into a wheelbarrow, bows his head, and gets to it while grumbling, "I don't know how I got roped into this."

A sentiment I understand too well. I would normally let Cordelia or someone else from the council handle festival preparation or cleanup. I'm only out here because of the nexus and making sure the magic is stable. Otherwise I wouldn't intentionally subject myself to Grammie Rae's ramblings about magic being her pal.

Then again—I force another swallow of coffee—I'm realizing all my careful research hasn't provided answers. More than a decade of studying magical theory, and nothing in my journals or notes or books explains what happens when Missy plays. It's not just when she's performing either. That kiss... something shifted when her lips met mine, as if the wards themselves held their breath. Magic isn't supposed to respond to emotion. It's equations, formulas, control.

But then why do I feel it pulse stronger whenever she—

A loud cheer cuts through the air. The high school baseball team has arrived, half of them wearing their caps, a few with younger brothers tagging along. Tom high-fives the kids from his team then pats the older boys on their shoulders.

This is what Tom wanted when he spoke to me—easy camaraderie, shared laughter, the simple joy of belonging.

Even after a decade here, I stand apart, more comfortable with ward lines than warm greetings. The Head Warlock isn't meant to be anyone's friend. That distance serves a purpose. In towns like Magnolia Cove, where enchantments thread through every streetlamp and sidewalk crack, the role demands restraint. Detachment. Control.

Or at least, it did before Missy started making me question everything I thought I understood about magic. And about connection.

The teenagers' arrival transforms the cleanup into something closer to organized chaos—hay bales become impromptu fortresses, leaves turn into ammunition.

Iris, who has spent the morning refreshing wilted flowers, ducks behind a display of chrysanthemums, giggling as Tom theatrically dodges her handful of maple leaves.

"Your aim is terrible!"

"Says the woman hiding behind flowers!"

I should probably stop them, insist on order and a good use of everyone's time. But even Grammie Rae has resigned herself to chuckling and rolling her eyes. I smile behind my coffee cup then the expression drops just as quickly.

I'm getting soft. Letting sentiment cloud judgment. Exactly what I promised myself I wouldn't do after—

"Good morning!"

Familiar laughter that makes my pulse skip accompanies Rachel's voice. Missy walks beside her and I'm not the only one who stopped by Ethan's bakery this morning. They both hold whisk-stamped coffee cups that curl steam into the cool post-storm air. Morning light makes Missy's hair gleam. The memory of how that hair felt twisted in my fingers during our storm-swept kiss sends electricity down my spine.

Rachel walks them closer to Tom and Iris, who are still laughing, a few leaves caught in their hair. Missy looks back. Catches my eye. Blushes so deeply the red spreads across her cheeks, reaching her ears. She shoots her attention back to the group but I'm frozen, unable to breathe.

"Well, well." Grammie Rae appears at my elbow, a butcher-knife-wide smile pasted on. "A little Magnolia Cove magic in the air, eh, oh mighty Head Warlock?"

My fingers tighten on the half-empty cup. "What do you mean by that?"

She shrugs but looks over to Missy who is, most unfortunately, looking back at me again. Grammie Rae's smile widens. "I told Ethan that the magic wanted her sister. It seems it's not satisfied with just one of them, though, does it?"

"*The Codex Arcanum* says nothing about magical preferences."

"*The Codex Arcanum*"—she stretches the words out and makes her voice high and formal—"was written by dusty old men." She elbows me, actually physically shoves her elbow into my ribs, which shocks me enough to hold back my retort. "The only thing they've ever kissed is their own asses. Unlike some people I could mention who were spotted kissing in the rain last night, eh?"

I choke on my coffee.

"Grammie Rae—"

"Oh, don't worry, honey. My lips are sealed." She mimes locking her mouth and throwing away the key, then winks at me. "You can't keep secrets from me, child, the magic tells me everything. And I have to say, it's about time someone made our stern Head Warlock blush and come up short on words. A bit of humility looks good on you."

Her words hit harder than her elbow. My coffee suddenly tastes bitter and filled with mint—with magic and the cost of it. The magic probably does tell her things. It's moody and mercurial, difficult to manage. They're practically a matched set. Nonetheless, I have a reputation to maintain here.

"I don't know what you think you saw—"

"Child,"—she cuts me off with another knowing smile—"I've lived with magic longer than you've been breathing. I know what it looks like when it finds something, or someone, it likes." She glances meaningfully at Missy, who's helping Emma tune her violin. "Just like I know what it looks like when someone's fighting something inevitable."

The protection pendant I'd spent half the night crafting as I waited out the storm shifts in my pocket, clinking softly against the old coin I always carry. Its magic hums against my leg, a quiet reminder of everything I'm supposed to protect. The idea had come to me after I'd returned home and started thinking about Missy, and the way she kisses like she plays, and how her music and touch steadies my magic and made it more manageable. More... alive.

Traditional wards fight against a magic being's unpredictable power, trying to contain it. But what if, like Missy's music, they could work with it instead? I'd infused the pendant with elements of harmony rather than control. I still hadn't decided if I'd give it to Emma yet, though.

Experimental magic should be documented, tested, and approved through proper channels. Not cobbled together in my study at midnight because a beautiful, passionate woman made me question everything I thought I knew about how my world works.

"The council has protocols," I manage, the words sounding hollow even to my own ears.

"The council,"—Grammie Rae pronounces each syllable like they offend her—"needs to get its collective head out of their musty books and remember that magic isn't just formulas and wards." She pats my arm. "It's alive, Dean. And right now, it's trying to tell you something. Maybe you should listen."

She bustles off toward Tom before I can formulate a response, leaving me with uncomfortable truths and cooling coffee. The worst part is, I'm starting to worry she might be right.

I find myself ignoring the controlled voice in my head and walking over to Missy and Emma, anyway.

"A good luck charm," I say, holding up the necklace, "for the Cove's star performer."

Emma's brow furrows at first. She reaches for the necklace, then pauses. But when she meets my gaze, she releases a breath and accepts the jewel, apparently understanding. She smooths a thumb over it as she turns to Missy. "Would you help me put it on?"

I hold my breath as Missy's fingers work the clasp. The stone glows subtly against Emma's skin, exactly as I'd expected. Perhaps those *dusty old books* had some benefit after all.

Emma twirls with her violin and drags the bow across the string. The note sings as she finds her seat for rehearsal. But Missy turns to face me.

"The stone was warm," she murmurs, looking up at me through long lashes.

I fight a groan. I can feel Grammie Rae's knowing gaze burning into my back. Despite her romantic ideals, I can't give Missy the truth. But I no longer wish to lie to her, either. "Sometimes things aren't what they seem."

Because the truth isn't safe in the hands of someone destined to leave. Missy's a performer—brilliant, bold, made for grand stages and faraway cities. She's not like her sister, who put down roots here and earned the right to carry the weight of our secrets. If Missy knew, really knew, it could put everyone at risk. Not because she's unkind or careless—but because her life isn't meant to stay contained. And magic this old, this hidden? It doesn't survive exposure.

Curiosity flashes across her eyes, darkening them. It's the same look her sister dons when she gets stubborn and fixed on an idea. But where Alex would push, Missy just shrugs. "Okay, then."

She takes a drink of her coffee and walks toward Rachel. Missy's lips curl around the lid, her throat bobbing as she swallows. The sight sends heat crawling up my neck. I force my attention back to ward lines, to duty, to anything but thinking about those lips and how they tasted against mine.

Later, as afternoon fades, the crowd disperses. I pretend to review the decorations once more while actually watching Missy say goodbye to Rachel. I expect her to leave next, but instead she walks over to me.

"So what exactly are you checking for the festival that takes you all day?"

"The grounds need special... preparations." The magic humming beneath our feet is nearly warm, stronger than I've ever felt it. "After the storm damage."

She frowns, a V-shaped furrow forming between her brows. "You were more honest with me last night."

The way she whispers the words, like a confession, cracks through me. "Missy, I wish I could... it's complicated."

"And at the Hoopla?" Her chin lifts stubbornly. "Will there be complicated things there I'll need to dance around as well?"

"If you want my honest opinion, then you should stay away from the festival." I step closer, betraying my own words. The air crackles between us like contained lightning. The more Missy tangles into our world, the more likely it is she'll start seeing the inevitable. And that would be bad for everyone involved.

And if that happens—if she glimpses something she isn't meant to—I'll be the one forced to wipe it away. I've used memory magic before. I've seen what it does to people when it's not well controlled, the fractures it leaves behind. I'd rather drain every last drop of power from my body than ever risk doing that to her.

"Is that what you want?" Her voice drops lower. "For me to stay away?"

The question hangs heavy with double meaning. We're alone on the festival grounds, magic pulsing beneath our feet, and the sunset painting everything in fire and shadow.

I can't lie to her any longer. I can't continue to pretend that everything in me doesn't long to capture her mouth with mine again, press her against me until she's fully aware of how much I want her to stay.

"No," I growl. "That's not what I want."

She closes the space between us in a moment. This kiss differs from our first—less hesitant. Her fingers curl into my shirt as mine trace the line of her jaw. When we finally break apart, reality crashes back.

"Missy, I…" I struggle to find the words, but they feel too heavy, too tangled. "This is also complicated."

Her eyes are piercing, soft but serious, but she tightens her grip. "Because you're on the council?"

I squeeze my eyes shut, hating the half-truth. "In a way, yes."

Some lies protect. Other destroy. I'm no longer sure which kind I'm telling.

"Then maybe," she whispers, "this doesn't have to be public." She smooths the wrinkles she's made in my shirt. "Maybe it could just be… ours. For now. If you're interested."

The word 'ours' settles in my chest like a spark looking for kindling. Dangerous. Warm. Inevitable.

"There's a trail," I find myself saying, "behind the old lighthouse. Nobody goes there this time of year."

A grin slips up her face, and her eyes sparkle. "I might need to practice there sometimes. For the album." She taps her chin and looks up at the darkening sky. "Perhaps around six tomorrow evening?"

"I might need to ensure the area is... secure... at that time."

Her grin widens even more. She walks away with measured steps, but glances back once. Just once. It's enough to undo every carefully constructed argument blaring in my head.

Grammie Rae's words echo in my mind. *The magic is alive, Dean. And right now, it's trying to tell you something.*

The wards pulse beneath my feet, stronger than they've been in years. Some part of me knows I'm standing at a crossroads—duty and desire, protocol and possibility. But maybe Grammie Rae is right. Maybe it's time to listen to what the magic's trying to tell me.

Even if what it's saying breaks every rule I've ever practiced.

Missy

I'm halfway to the lighthouse when I realize how ridiculous this is. Giuseppe's case bumps against my leg with each step, a steady reminder that I don't know what I'm doing. The weight of my phone in my pocket feels heavier than my cello—filled with Jules' increasingly frustrated messages about the album's timeline and my radio silence.

I haven't answered yet. I keep telling myself I'm just taking a breath, just buying time. But the longer I'm here in Magnolia Cove—surrounded by stillness and cinnamon and space to think—the harder it is to imagine going back.

Not that I'd ever admit that. Not even to myself.

"Just leaving to work on my composition," I'd told Alex when I'd left, the lie bitter on my tongue. She'd been elbow-deep in dough, hair dusted with flour, looking so content it made my chest ache. "Quiet helps, and Rachel said I could use the studio whenever I like."

"It's so great you and Rachel get along."

My stomach swooped with the deceit. I've never outright lied to my sister. Misleading her on the state of my happiness I practiced often enough, but this was unfamiliar territory.

"Yeah, it's great."

My face had to have paled. Blood tingled as it rushed away from it. Alex narrowed her eyes at me then gave her head a shake and grinned. "Sometimes I still forget you're an adult." She chuckled. "Want some snacks for the road? I think I've finally nailed this caramel apple biscotti."

I'd accepted the paper bag, my stomach churning but not with hunger. Alex sacrificed everything to give me my perfect life, and here I am sneaking around like a teenager with a crush —avoiding the work I keep insisting I'm doing, and seriously considering quitting the very career she helped me build.

And I don't even know how to explain why.

I squeeze my eyes shut for a moment, grip Giuseppe's case strap tighter, and blow out a breath.

No, it's fine. I'm not giving up my career—I can't—and I'm not marrying Dean just because we're going to have a little fall fling. I'll get it out of my system, regain my spark, and be traveling the world again by this time next year.

Because I have to.

Alex gave up everything to make this life possible for me— her savings, her dreams, years of her life. If I walk away now, it's not just a career I'm quitting. It's her sacrifice I'm throwing away.

And I couldn't live with that.

The path winds through trees painted in autumn's palette —rust and amber mixing with pine green. Summer's breathed its last, and winter will arrive soon. One more season in Magnolia Cove. The thought sends an unexpected pang through my chest.

When I round the last bend, Dean's already there. He's traded his usual leather jacket for a dark sweater and jeans, and something about seeing him in more casual clothing makes my heart flutter. Maybe because it's like seeing behind a curtain, like being trusted with something rare.

"You showed up." The words slip out before I can stop them.

His lips quirk. "Said I would, didn't I?"

"You said maybe."

"Maybe means yes when it's you asking."

The honesty in his voice draws me forward until I'm close enough to feel the heat radiating from his body. When I kiss him, it's hesitant initially—still unsure if this is allowed. His hands slide down to my waist, splaying gently at first, like he's giving me the chance to pull away. But I don't. Instead, I lean in, letting the kiss deepen as his touch becomes firmer, more certain. The rhythmic breathing of the ocean and the wind rattling pine needles fades—everything does except for the press of his lips and the quiet heat building between us.

Dean pulls back first. He drags his knuckles down my jaw and my core turns into molten lava. His gaze flicks to Giuseppe's case. "Brought company?"

"Didn't know if I'd end up spending the hour playing alone." It comes out more vulnerable than I intend and I fight a cringe.

He catches my hand, though, his fingers warm and rough. "Come with me? I'd like to show you something."

I nod, not trusting my voice. He leads me to the lighthouse door, producing a key from his pocket. Inside, the space opens up like a music box someone's just wound. A spiral staircase curves toward the light above and aging posters of whales and mermaids cover pale-blue walls. When Dean clicks on strings of lights, the whole room transforms. They cast star-like patterns across the walls, making impressions like raindrops or galaxies.

"Twinkle lights? Really?" I can't help but tease, but my heart squeezes at this glimpse behind his carefully constructed walls. The space feels lived in, personal in a way his stark office doesn't. I try to picture him here alone, maybe reading or watching the waves. How many other people know this side of him? How many others has he invited here? Something tells me the answer is very few, which makes this moment feel precious.

He raises an eyebrow, but there's a softness to his expression. "String lights take batteries which is practical in a place without electricity. But that's not what I wanted to show you."

He releases a shaky breath then cranks open a window. Salt air mingles with the sound of waves, allowing in nature's rhythm. But he's still moving with nervous energy, adjusting things on an old desk like he's working up to something.

I've never seen Dean in any way less than completely composed—even during our heated kiss in the storm, he maintained that careful control. But now his fingers tap against his leg, and there's something almost fragile in the way he won't quite meet my eyes.

I want to reach for him, to ease whatever's making him nervous, but I stay still. This feels like watching a wild animal slowly venture closer—one wrong move and he might retreat behind those walls again. So I wait, letting the sound of the ocean breathing fill the silence between us. Whatever he wants to show me clearly matters, and I realize I want to be worthy of the trust he's placing in me.

Finally, he sighs and pulls a guitar case from behind a cabinet.

I can't help myself. My hands actually clap together of their own accord. "You're going to play for me?"

His jaw works, his eyes tightening and growing dark, and his voice is gruff when he speaks. "I said I might one day." His tone softens as he raises his face. "And as I told you earlier, 'maybe' tends to mean 'yes' when it's you asking."

There's something so vulnerably honest about his words,

about the way he's looking at me now—like I'm something precious and terrifying all at once. It reminds me of how I feel before stepping onto a stage, that moment of standing on the edge of something transformative. But this isn't a performance. This is Dean, letting his guard down note by note, and somehow that feels more momentous than any concert I've ever given.

"Do you have a second chair?" I nod toward the desk's lonely seat. "I'd love to join you, I mean, if you wanted that."

He produces a folded chair from a closet, and we set up our instruments like we're preparing for a private concert. When I tell him to play whatever he wants, that I'll follow, something vulnerable flashes across his face.

The song he starts is raw—all minor chords and emotional wounds turned into music. I close my eyes and let Giuseppe's voice join, not thinking about proper finger positions or Jules' careful notations or what anyone else would expect. For once, I'm just playing.

Our instruments seem to know each other, like they've waited for this duet. The lighthouse's acoustics turn every sound into something magical, better than any concert hall I've ever played.

Playing with Jules is like walking a tightrope—every note precisely balanced, each melody a complex dance where one misstep could send us tumbling. He's brilliant, of course. A virtuoso. But sometimes it feels like we're two separate performers sharing a stage rather than actually making music together.

This is different. Dean might not have Jules' technical perfection, but his playing has something more vital—a raw honesty that makes my breath catch. His simple melodies speak straight to the heart. For the first time in years, I'm not worried about perfection. I'm just letting music flow through me, letting Giuseppe's voice twine with Dean's guitar in ways that feel natural and free. There's no pressure to impress, no need to prove anything. Just two people sharing pieces of themselves through music.

When we finish, I realize my cheeks are wet. I blink lingering tears away and lift my face. Dean notices too. His smile is soft, private—a kind that I can't imagine he shares very often.

"Another?" I ask, already knowing his answer in my bones.

This, I realize as we start our next piece, *this is the magic I've been searching for.* Not in perfect performances or critical acclaim, but in the space between notes where two people choose to be real together.

The biscotti sits forgotten in its paper bag, and my phone stays untouched in my pocket. I'm grateful that the island's terrible service means Jules' messages can't reach me here. For now, there's just music and Dean and the way the twinkle lights glisten across his eyes and reflect on his guitar's polished surface, turning ordinary wood into something almost magical in the dim light.

Once the sun has painted the lighthouse walls gold, and our instruments are safely packed away, Dean pulls me close for one more kiss. It's softer than our earlier ones, like he's memorizing the moment.

"What are the chances you're free at the same time tomorrow?" he asks against my hair.

My heart does the fluttery thing again. There's basically nothing that could keep me from coming again, from feeling this way, from finding out what other secrets this lighthouse—and its keeper—holds. "I might be able to clear my schedule."

He laughs—actually laughs—and the sound is better than any music we made. "Wouldn't want to impede on the important schedule of master cellist, Margaret Sinclair."

"Oh, I wouldn't want to impose on your important council duties either. I'm sure you have urgent pumpkin inspections for the Hoopla. Or perhaps some teenage musicians to intimidate with your stern glares?"

He laughs again, softer this time. "Is that a yes or a maybe?"

"It's an 'I should probably use the time to respond to Jules' emails and pretend I'm working on our album' but it's a 'yes' if you're the one asking."

His arms tighten. "How is that going?"

"The working or the pretending?"

"Either. Both."

I think about the unfinished compositions waiting in my room, how for the first time since Juilliard I'm not sure I want the future I've planned. But Dean's looking at me like I'm something precious, and the setting sun is turning everything to magic, and somehow none of those complications seem to matter.

"Ask me tomorrow." I stretch up for one last kiss.

As I walk home through growing shadows, Giuseppe's case bumps against my legs and I realize I'm humming something new. Not a carefully crafted melody, but something wild and honest and entirely my own.

I'm nearly to the lighthouse again, Giuseppe's familiar weight against my leg no longer feeling like guilt but anticipation. These past two weeks have settled into a pleasant rhythm. My days start with early before-school practices with Emma. Rachel and Dean usually observe. I try not to steal glances at Dean, at least not obviously. In the afternoon, I help Alex around the store and get to sample Zoe's increasingly eccentric wedding treat ideas. Yesterday's was lavender-matcha-rose macaroons and I still can't decide if I loved or hated them. And my evenings—those stolen moments—feel more real than any stage I've ever played on.

Jules' messages pile up in my inbox like fallen leaves, but I can't bring myself to care. The music flowing through me now isn't his carefully constructed masterpieces. It's powerful and untethered and I can't stop following it now. I tell myself that's why Giuseppe still accompanies me everywhere, though it's just as much about maintaining the fiction Alex and Ethan believe—that I'm frequently slipping away to private practice sessions. The lie sits lighter these days, though my stomach still aches a bit when I think about it.

Dean's waiting when I round the last bend, the setting sun painting him in shades of autumn. He rolls his sleeves and runs a hand through his hair, then drums his fingers nervously against his leg. When he spots me, his shoulders tense then forcibly relax, like he's trying to maintain control but can't quite manage it. My heart skips a beat. This is new.

When he kisses me hello, even that feels different. An urgency breaks through his usual measured restraint. His fingers tremble slightly as they fumble with the lighthouse key, and he has to clear his throat before speaking. "I brought something today. To make things more... comfortable."

The door creaks open on our private world and I catch my breath. In our usual corner, Dean has created a nest of thick blankets and pillows, surrounded by even more twinkle lights. He moves around the room, turning them all on so that stars dance along the weathered walls and glisten over the plush comforters.

He shuffles around and straightens an already perfect blanket. I fight back a laugh. This man who maintains iron control over an entire town is fidgeting like a nervous teenager, and somehow that makes me feel completely certain.

Setting Giuseppe down with careful reverence, I grab Dean's hand and pull him toward the makeshift bed. I kick off my shoes and sink into the softness, drawing him with me. Above us, the spiral staircase winds toward windows painted in sunset colors, and salt air mingles with the sound of waves.

Every day the sun sets a little earlier, the dark comes a bit sooner.

"Can I ask you something?" Dean's voice is raspy against my hair.

"Of course." I trace patterns on his arm, marveling at how natural this feels.

"Why do you avoid the work you're doing with Jules if you love what you do and you're so good at it?"

I take a breath, searching for the truth. It's something I've been avoiding answering myself. "I've seen Jules literally miss an entire night's sleep perfecting a song and take the stage the next evening just as energized as ever. He's brilliant at it. But I..." For a moment I pause, the crashing waves filling my quiet. Dean's embrace tightens, but he doesn't interrupt. "I just want to play from my heart," I say. "That's not how it works in that world, though. Everything has to be precise, planned a year in advance, perfect."

Dean's thumb brushes circles on my arm, and something about it grounds me as I continue. "And Alex is so proud of who I've become. You don't know what all she sacrificed for me to get here. How do I tell her I might want something different?"

Dean's quiet for a long moment, his fingers drawing abstract patterns along my side. "I might understand that part more than you think," he finally says, voice rough.

I hesitate, then gather my courage. "Your sister?" I whisper, the question I've wanted to ask for weeks. "I've noticed you don't talk about her. Is she...?" I let the question hang, afraid to assume the worst.

He presses a kiss to the top of my head. "She's alive. Her wedding is coming up, actually. My mother sent an invitation but..." He releases a heavy breath. "I broke her heart once. She hasn't spoken to me since. Some things can't be fixed."

"How long has it been?"

"More than a decade."

"What?" I sit up and stare at him, pressing my palms against his sculpted chest. "Over ten years? Dean, that's—" I stop myself from saying 'ridiculous' and soften my voice instead. "Have you tried reaching out? People change. Hearts heal."

He kisses me, soft and slow, then offers a sad smile. "Thank you for caring. But, you don't know my sister. It's impossible." Before I can protest his lips are on mine, gentle still but urgent. "Besides," he whispers against them, "she's not who I'm wanting to talk about right now."

There's a part of me that wants to press him for more about his sister. But the heat that pools in my body at his touch, the electric sizzle that seems to spark between us entirely drowns out that voice.

I kiss him instead. It turns deep and urgent. His hands slide down my curves and my fingers explore his shoulders then find his sweater's hem. I hesitate for just a moment before slipping my hand under, savoring the warmth of his skin.

He inhales sharply at my touch, his muscles tensing then relaxing under my fingertips. The sweater lifts away like a whispered crescendo, revealing a lean, muscled torso. My breath catches as I take in the sight of him. Dean's always handsome, but like this—hair mussed, eyes dark with wanting, chest rising and falling rapidly—he's breathtaking.

"Missy," he breathes against my neck, his voice as rough as I've ever heard it. "Are you sure? I know I set this up in here but we don't have to if you don't want—"

"I want to." I've never felt more sure of anything. "Please, Dean."

The sound he makes against my skin resonates through me like the lowest note on Giuseppe's strings. His hands map my body with reverent precision, each touch an exploration of dynamics—soft then urgent, gentle then demanding as he peels clothes away. When our eyes meet, the intensity in his gaze steals my breath. I've seen that look before, during the storm when thunder cracked around us and lightning painted his features in stark relief. But there's no storm to blame for the electricity crackling between us, no thunder to drown out my racing heart.

His fingers trace the curve of my neck, like he's memorizing sheet music. His lips follow, and I arch into his touch, wanting more. The way he holds me—like I'm something precious yet unbreakable, makes me feel both powerful and vulnerable. My hands find their way to his hair, gripping, and the sound he makes vibrates into my skin.

"Wait," he murmurs, pressing a kiss to my temple before reaching for his wallet. Even this moment feels charged with meaning—his care, his protection.

Then we're creating our own symphony, every touch an arpeggio, every kiss a crescendo. The twinkle lights cast their spell across his skin, turning our private concert into something sacred. His hands map my body like he's discovering a new instrument, learning which touches draw sighs, which caresses make me gasp.

I've performed in the world's greatest concert halls, but nothing has ever felt as perfectly orchestrated as this—the way we move together, the rhythm we create, the harmonies we build. At this moment, there's no need for precision or technical mastery. Just the pure music of two hearts finding their shared melody.

Later, wrapped in blankets and starlight, reality seeps back in. "I should go soon," I mumble. "Before Alex worries."

Dean pulls me closer but sighs against my shoulder. "You probably should."

"Dean..." I hesitate. Swallow. Force myself to be brave and say the words. "I can't keep pretending this is just..."

"I know." His arm tightens.

"It's complicated, I remember."

He's quiet for a long moment and I match my breathing to the waves. Before he speaks again, he presses a kiss to my shoulder. "If I asked you to trust me, to give me some time, and I promise I'll explain everything—would you?"

The lights dance across the beaten walls. I nestle my face into the blanket's warmth and breathe in Dean's cinnamon and salt scent, letting the familiar mixture settle my racing thoughts. Trust has always been complicated for me. I've spent so many years being what others needed, measuring my worth in perfect performances and meeting expectations. But Dean... Dean sees past the polished exterior to the messy, uncertain woman beneath. He's never asked me to be anything but exactly who I am.

"Yes," I whisper, surprised by how easily the word comes. Like the natural resolution of a complex chord progression, like finding the perfect note after searching through endless variations. "I can do that."

As we dress, his hand lingers on my cheek with a tenderness that has me holding my breath. For the first time, I let myself imagine building a future here—not just with Dean, but in Magnolia Cove. Teaching music, writing my own songs, creating something true.

We part ways as always—walking back on separate paths. But tonight, something shifts in me like a key change in a familiar melody. I turn back, drawn by an impulse I don't resist, and find him still standing in the gathering dusk, watching me go.

The way he looks at me—unguarded, longing, real— mirrors everything that thrums through my skin. We've crossed some invisible threshold, moved beyond the realm of stolen moments and secret smiles into something deeper.

The composition of us has shifted—evolved into something too powerful to contain in mere snippets of stolen time. There's no more pretending this isn't changing us both.

Dean

The autumn spice cookies weigh like stones in their box, each step toward the planetarium a study in controlled panic. Mom's care package had arrived this morning—her continuing to reach across the divide I'd created. The scent of cinnamon and clove wraps around memories of home, reminding me of simpler times filled with pillow forts and shared laughter. Back before magic kindled our destruction.

Now magic sparks differently. It hums beneath my feet with each step, responding to thoughts of Missy in ways that defy every law I've spent years mastering.

Yesterday, I'd asked the council's permission to share our truth with Missy—with Margaret Sinclair, that was. I'd maintained my carefully constructed mask of detachment all while my heart thundered treacherously within my chest. I'd already told Missy I'd give her the truth. What if they didn't agree?

I'd laid the arguments out logically: she had an extended stay which she was bound to repeat in the future, her sister already knew, and she was a person with unusual sensitivity to magical energies. My voice never wavered. Yet, Eleanor had winked at me when she'd voted in favor.

"Some humans handle the truth well," she'd said after the meeting finished and I had permission. "Look at Alex."

But Alex had discovered magic through Ethan—had fallen in love with him before learning what he was. Missy... Missy already has one foot out the door, another tour on the horizon. She's ignoring those things, but I'd be foolish to discount them. To not recognize that her time here has an expiration date. Missy isn't her sister. She probably wouldn't choose to stay. Frankly, she's too talented to waste it here. Even if she isn't satisfied with her current career, another path will open. And I don't doubt she'll walk it.

The setting sun paints the planetarium's dome in amber and rose. Missy stands silhouetted against it, her dress catching the wind like music made visible. She's wearing her hair down tonight, loose tresses dancing in the breeze.

Something inside me aches at the sight of her. How many nights have we spent in shadows, stealing moments between sunset and sunrise? As if this—as if she—were something to hide.

She turns at my approach and her smile steals my carefully rehearsed words.

"I have a question," she says.

I kiss her softly, grateful for any excuse to delay what is coming. "Nothing new there."

She slaps my arm playfully, then rests her fingers against my bicep in a way that makes me want to forget everything except the way her touch ignites something primal and desperate in me, how her fingers leave trails of heat through my shirt that make me forget I'm supposed to be the controlled one, the responsible one, the one who maintains order rather than shattering it with kisses that taste like midnight confessions and barely restrained magic.

"Hey." She laughs. "You like my questions."

"I like the one doing the questioning."

Her scowl is adorably indignant. She props her hands on her hips. "Why would an island that runs on tourism have an observatory and not have it open for tours or shows?"

The playfulness drains from me. She's cutting right to the heart of why I brought her here, this woman who sees too much and questions everything. I slip the key from my pocket and try to maintain my composure, but my voice is rough when I answer. "I promise I'll answer that in a few minutes."

She sinks down off her tiptoes, back to earth. That's where she's about to land—in reality. Likely one that will have her running fast and far, back to concert halls and standing ovations and a life untouched by the complications of magic. Back to a world where mysterious observatories stay locked and a man she's interested in isn't tied to the mercurial magic system of a small island. A world where Dean Markham was just a small town bureaucrat rather than the keeper of secrets that could shatter her reality.

I take my time shifting the key into place. I've unlocked this door hundreds of times, but never with stakes that felt so personal. Never with my heart hammering against my ribs like it might break free, never with magic crackling beneath my skin in response to her mere presence.

She follows me inside. Instead of pressing for answers immediately she looks up at the glass panes that showcase the sky's transformation—twilight bleeding from lavender to indigo, the first stars piercing through in pinpricks against velvet.

She laughs again, throws her head back and arms out, and spins in a circle, her dress twirling around her legs. Joy radiates from her like its own kind of magic. That is her gift. She can scoop happiness out of sidewalk cracks and dusty corners. God knows she's somehow excavated it from me.

I want to kiss her. I want to lock the door, peel away her clothes, and worship every inch of her skin. I want to sit and listen to her talk about music for hours. By all the wards below, I want to let my guitar's clumsy chords twine with her cello's expertly tuned voice again. To feel that inexplicable surge when our instruments sync and my magic feels like it's found its missing half—raw and wild and perfect. Music has always been my singular sanctuary, my secret rebellion against the rigid constraints. But with Missy, it's become something else entirely. Something that feels like possibility.

"You've wanted answers." The words come out steadier than I feel. Missy goes still, her perceptive eyes turning toward me. She nods but doesn't speak, like she's holding space for me to continue. "When your sister first found out, Ethan told her I was there in case anything went wrong." I swallow hard, shoving my trembling hands into my pockets. "That's my actual role here, Missy. I'm the one who's there if things go wrong and that's still true. If this is too much, or you feel nervous, just say the word and—"

Horror sweeps up my throat, clogging the words. I'm essentially offering to use memory magic on her—the very thing that shattered my relationship with Nell. Magic that, wielded carelessly, leaves scars deeper than physical wounds. I've seen it happen. I've *caused* it.

Missy's giggle shatters my spiral of self-recrimination. "Alex *is* part of a cult, isn't she?"

"A cult?"

"Magnolia Cove. I'm pretty sure I've seen this movie, actually. Cute town, handsome scowl-y leader, adorable shops but—"

"We're not a cult." I don't know how she does this—how she takes the weight of decades and makes it feel as insubstantial as dandelion fluff. I'm smiling. I'm about to do the most terrifying thing in my life and I'm smiling. "And if you believe I'm the leader of a cult, then you shouldn't have followed me to an isolated observatory right before it gets dark."

Her lips curve into a grin that never fails to undo me. "I've been meeting you alone at a lighthouse for weeks."

"That would be..." I clear my throat, fighting both another grin and the memory of her skin dappled in the glow of twinkle lights. "Also ill-advised."

"I'd like to think Alex would warn me if I were in real danger." She steps closer, close enough that I catch some sweet smell that isn't normally on her. Probably something Alex was baking.

"Unless our cult has brainwashed her." The words slip out as dry as autumn leaves, surprising a laugh from her.

"All right, if you're not a cult, then what are you?"

The moment stretches between us like a held breath. I study her face and try to memorize how she looks in this liminal space between before and after. The last seconds where she still sees me as just a man rather than a warlock. Where magic is still a metaphor rather than reality. Where everything between us exists in that perfect space of possibility, before truth reshapes it all.

My fingers flex at my sides, magic building beneath my skin like a gathering storm. One gesture and I'll change everything. One moment of power and I could lose her forever.

I've done this before. And I lost, then.

But Missy deserves more than half-truths and shadows. More than stolen moments in lighthouses and careful deflections. She deserves to choose this—or not choose it—with her eyes wide open. That thought steadies my shaking hands. This isn't about my fears anymore. It's about giving her the truth she should have had weeks ago, before the first kiss in the rain, before the lighthouse, before blankets and pillows beneath twinkle lights, before I let myself fall.

I reach for my magic—the power that's always hummed beneath my skin, stronger than most. Slowly, I lift my hand and offer it to her, palm up between us. Magic doesn't require gestures. Not really. But we teach them to children as a way to focus, to ground, to steady the surge of power.

Apparently, at this moment, I need the crutch too.

Stars bloom around us, constellations dancing in the air. Comets streak past her shoulders, their light playing across her skin and making her eyes shimmer with a soft, ethereal glow.

I brace for her scream. For her stumbling away from me. For the terror that will force me to become everything I swore I'd never be again. And I'll have to be the one to clean it up. I'd already committed to the council that I'd handle it and—

Missy laughs. She reaches out to touch a star, and it sizzles around her fingers. "This is magic," she whispers, then looks at me with wonder in her eyes. "This is real magic?"

"Yes." I retreat to a one-word answer, gruffly spoken and tensed muscles. I was prepared for fear, for betrayal, for panic.

But joy? I don't know what to do with joy.

Missy reaches for another star but her gaze slips backs to my face. She lowers her hand. "Or, is it not? Real, I mean."

"It's real."

"The entire town?"

"Runs on magic, yes."

"And your actual job is?"

I swallow hard, hands fisted in my pockets. Here's the moment of truth. "Head Warlock of Magnolia Cove."

She mouths the word 'warlock,' eyes wide. I steel myself. I'm a complicated person to imagine dating even for magical beings—most find my power intimidating, my dedication to rules frustrating. For a human musician who values freedom and creativity, who still has an entire world of stages and spotlights ahead of her...

She crosses to me and presses her lips against mine. I'm almost afraid to touch her, certain this can't be real. The shock will wear off. The panic will come.

"Missy, aren't you afraid?"

She looks up at me, mischief and starlight dancing in her eyes. "Would it make you feel better if I was? I'm a mediocre actress but I'll give it a try."

Her eyes go comically wide as she clutches her hand to her chest. "Oh no," she gasps with all the dramatic flair of the lead actress in a middle school play. "Magic! How terrifying! What shall I do?" She pretends to swoon, then ruins the effect by giggling. "Was that scared enough? I can try screaming if you'd prefer, but the acoustics in here seem excellent. I'd hate to deafen you."

The laugh that bursts from me feels like breaking chains. I pull her into my arms, spinning her through starlight until we're both dizzy with it.

We end up on the floor by the telescope, my back against the wall and Missy curled against my chest. I tell her everything I can—how Magnolia Cove's food and scenery pulse with magic that subtly enhances them, how wards keep most humans from noticing but there are exceptions like her and Alex, how we have an observatory because magic runs on seasonal changes and planetary alignment. While she was studying music theory in college, I was learning astrology and magical law.

I explain about Emma, about magical children who can't leave magical pocket communities unless they master their powers. How there are some members of our community who want to see her rise into magical leadership, but I don't want that forced on her. I want her to follow her passion if possible. But sometimes, for people like us, magical beings who can access so much, it isn't possible.

"When did you start playing?" she asks, fingers tracing patterns on my arm.

"After my magic manifested. My parents thought learning to resonate with it might help me control my powers." I offer a half-smile at the memory. It didn't help as much as they'd hoped, but maybe they were on to something. Missy's playing certainly steadies my abilities. "I mostly used it to annoy Nell with terrible covers."

"I can't imagine you playing terrible covers."

"I was very committed to being misunderstood."

Her laughs make the stars dance, and I wonder what she does to the magic. About all the things I don't know. About the future she's opened up to me I've never considered before. Her next question makes my breath catch, though.

"Was that why you couldn't tell me before? About Nell? Because whatever happened involved magic?"

I force myself to meet her gaze. "Yes. Nell fell in love with a human her senior year of high school. He had a... normal reaction to learning about magic."

"Oh?" Her lips twitch. "You mean he didn't give you an amateur dramatic performance?"

"Your acting is terrible," I say, but then the humor drains from my voice. "He panicked. Spread the information quickly. Our Head Warlock was away, and we didn't have time for a careful solution." I pause, jaw tightening. "You have to understand—when word gets out about magic, it never ends well. Humans don't typically respond with wonder. They respond with fear. And fear turns into control. Containment. Violence."

I meet her eyes. "We've seen it happen across continents, across centuries. One town whispers about miracles, and the next week they're burning witches or jailing anyone with magical affinity." I pause, the words bitter on my tongue and tainted with the sting of mint-flavored memory magic. "We can't risk exposure... even if it came from the person my sister was dating."

Understanding dawns in her eyes. "They asked you to handle it?"

I swallow hard. Nod. "I was twenty and barely learning to

control my power." A bitter laugh escapes. "Sometimes I think I may never truly master it. I needed to use memory magic, but I... I cut too deep. Instead of erasing specific memories, I took years. Nell lost her entire circle of friends in one night. Because of me."

"Dean." She touches my cheek, her fingers impossibly gentle. "That wasn't your fault. You were practically a kid, and others made those decisions. You did the best you could."

I brush hair back from her forehead, marveling at how she can take a decade of guilt and make it feel lighter. "Maybe. But I broke my sister's heart. I had migraines for weeks after using that much high-level magic. When I finally came out of the haze, I saw what I'd done to her. She didn't just lose her boyfriend—she lost her entire world. Her friends didn't recognize her anymore. How do you come back from that?"

She leans into my touch, starlight still gleaming in her eyes. "Maybe you start by forgiving yourself."

The simple words hit harder than any magical act. I pull her closer, breathing in her sweet scent and press a kiss to the top of her head. I'd love to imagine a world that's as simple and trusting as her words. It doesn't exist, though. Nell made it clear the last time I saw her that the only road to healing for her was to never see me again.

"Playing the guitar is something you did with Nell?" she asks, whisper soft.

"Yes." My voice has gone hoarse. She's dredging up painful memories long buried, but I somehow know she'll handle them with care.

"I didn't realize what a gift you'd given me when you shared your playing, Dean. Thank you." I look down at her and kiss her. She sighs before speaking again. "Maybe playing more could be the first step to forgiving yourself."

"Maybe."

She smiles, but it's gentle. "Do you think you might play more, then?"

"Only for you."

The words slip out raw, and honest, like everything about us has become. Maybe she has a point. Getting to know her has changed me—changed how I see myself. The rigid walls I've maintained, the isolation I've chosen, it all seems less necessary now.

Maybe I'm becoming something new. A caterpillar ready to wake with new wings.

Missy

The biscotto melts on my tongue, rich with almond and something else—something that makes the flavors brighter, more alive. I've noticed that about the food in Magnolia Cove today. Maybe it's because I know about magic now, or maybe it's just that everything tastes better when you're happy.

I curl my fingers around my teacup and watch steam rise in lazy spirals. If I unfocus my eyes just right, and fight the urge to look away, I can almost see it—that slight shimmer in the air that Dean explained is magic. It's like heat waves rising from summer pavement, but more deliberate somehow. More alive.

It's everywhere in Magnolia Cove once you know to look for it. In the way the autumn leaves dance a little too perfectly, how every slice of pie tastes a bit like comfort, how even the simplest cup of tea seems to warm you from the inside out.

Dean.

The memory of him in the planetarium hits me fresh. Constellations dancing around us as he finally shared his truth. The raw vulnerability in his eyes as he waited for me to run screaming. As if I could ever be afraid of him. Even knowing what he can do now—stop other magical beings from accessing their powers, alter memories, and infuse magic into the wards that keep Magnolia Cove secret—it only makes me trust him more. Because he holds that power carefully, uses it only to protect.

I get why others find him intimidating. The stern expression, the rigid posture, the way he seems to see straight through pretense. But they don't know how his eyes soften when he plays guitar, the lilt of his laughter when he really means it, or how gentle his hands can be when they're mapping constellations across my skin.

Alex hums behind the counter, greeting regulars as the bell chimes their arrival. She's really in her element here, in this cafe that somehow manages to be both sleek and cozy. I need to tell her tonight. On our walk home, I'll explain about Dean. About how I know about magic now. About how I think I might be falling—

No. Not thinking. Fallen. Completely, irrevocably fallen for the man everyone else tiptoes around.

I take another sip of tea, letting the warmth settle into my bones. It should terrify me, how much has changed. How different my future might look from the one I'd carefully orchestrated. A few months ago, I was Margaret Sinclair, cello prodigy, watching the future unfold like sheet music—each note precisely where it should be. Now I'm just Missy, sitting in my sister's cafe, contemplating magic and watching leaves dance when they shouldn't, and feeling more real than I ever did on stage. The only thing I feel is peace.

The bell chimes again.

"Maestro! Your audience awaits!"

That familiar voice cuts through my contentment like a bow shrieking across strings. Jules stands in the doorway, violin case slung over his shoulder, looking every inch the star performer in his tailored velvet blazer and hand stitched shoes.

His wild grin flashes and his emerald eyes sparkle in the golden lights of the shop.

Jules, here? The realization hits me with the force of a missed entrance, setting my heart racing like a tempo marking I can't quite follow. I must have ignored my inbox more thoroughly than I thought to have missed this—Jules Bouchard voluntarily coming to Magnolia Cove, the place he'd once described as 'where careers go to die.'

My stomach drops as I think of the still unfinished compositions gathering dust in my room, the album deadlines I've dodged like water balloons. The life I've built here suddenly feels fragile, like a delicate crescendo about to shatter. I've been living in a different time signature entirely, losing myself in lighthouse melodies and magical moments while Jules has undoubtedly been crafting our future with his usual precision.

Oh god. My heart seizes even as I rise to my feet. I should have worked more. Should have at least maintained the pretense of progress. Instead, I've been discovering a completely different music, one that has nothing to do with perfect performances and everything to do with raw, honest emotion.

Still muscle memory is a powerful thing. As he strides toward me, arms thrown wide, I fall into the familiar choreography of our friendship. Like a well-rehearsed duet, my body remembers its part even as my mind stumbles over the changed melody of my heart. Hugging Jules feels like hitting play on an old favorite song. Maybe I wouldn't pick it anymore, but there's still something nostalgic about it when it comes on.

"What are you doing here?" I ask against his neck.

His embrace carries the ghost of a hundred post-performance celebrations, the echo of late-night rehearsals and shared triumphs that once defined my world. I breathe him in, because there is comfort in the familiar. Even if familiar smells like posh bergamot and oak-moss cologne.

"Visiting my wayward cellist, of course!" His laugh resonates with that particular Jules cadence—part showman, part conspirator. His grip tightens and he whispers, "This autumn has been unbearably dull without you, Missy."

He lifts me off my feet until I laugh, another familiar gesture that suddenly feels wrong instead of reassuring. Only as Jules sets me down does my world tilt on its axis. There, framed in the doorway like a stark charcoal sketch against autumn light, stands Dean.

His face is a careful blank canvas, the kind he wears when answering people's requests to bend the rules. But I know him well enough now to read the subtle tells—the tick in his jaw, the way his shoulders have gone rigid, and the tight clench of his teeth like he's biting back words he doesn't trust himself to say.

I'm achingly aware of every point of contact where Jules still touches me. My skin feels too tight, like a cello string wound past its breaking point. At this moment, my two worlds aren't just colliding—they're shattering against each other.

Dean's dark eyes meet mine for just a heartbeat, but in that fragment of time, I see something I've never witnessed there before: uncertainty. It flickers across his carefully composed features like a shadow across water, there and gone so quickly I might have imagined it. But I know I haven't. Just as I know that the careful walls he's lowered for me these past weeks are rising again, brick by brick, with every second Jules' hands linger on my shoulders.

I want to run to Dean. To explain that this isn't what it looks like. But Jules is already talking rapid fire and I can't get my brain to think.

"The recording studio in Vienna is holding our slot

through December—" His fingers tap a rhythm against my shoulder and I realize he's still touching me. "Absolute miracle, considering their waitlist. But when I played them the rough cut of your solo in the third movement—"

I catch the exact moment Dean turns away. The space he leaves feels hollow, a music box without its melody.

"—and Marketing thinks we can leverage your 'small-town sabbatical' angle. Very relatable, very human interest—" Jules' hand still rests on me, heavy as a judge's verdict. "The critics are already buzzing about our bold artistic evolution—"

His energy hums like he's downed a trio of espressos before striding in here, but I feel like the breath has been stolen from me. I'm not sure he's even realized I've yet to reply to a thing he's said.

Alex wipes her hands on a tea towel and walks from behind the counter. She smiles as she reaches out her hand. "Mr. Bouchard, great to meet you again."

"Jules, please." His smile shifts to something warmer, less performative. "And your cafe is absolutely enchanting. The exposed brick, the lighting—" He gestures with elegant fingers, finally dragging them away from me. "Like a piece of Manhattan tucked away in paradise."

I remember once he'd referred to Magnolia Cove as a 'cultural wasteland.' The memory sits sour in my mind.

"Where are you staying?" Alex flicks the towel over her shoulder.

"The most darling inn just up the hill." Jules' eyes sparkle. "Though I must say the decor is.... enthusiastic. I'm sharing my room with no less than three different floral patterns on the walls alone, not counting the bedspread or the dozen framed botanical prints. I believe I've reached my quota of roses for the year."

"A shame," I hear myself say, "considering how many bouquets you get after performances."

His laugh carries the theatrical quality that used to make my heart flutter. "Too true, darling. Too true."

"Oh yes," Alex says, "That's where I stayed the first time I visited The Cove, as well. Mrs. Haversham is lovely."

They continue chatting, their voices weaving together like a familiar duet, but I'm suddenly aware of every discordant note in my life's composition. I haven't told Jules about potentially leaving touring. I haven't told Alex about Dean. I haven't told Dean about Jules trying to push our relationship beyond professional. I've been living in a bubble that's about to pop.

Alex's brow furrows as she picks up on my expression. Jules doesn't seem to notice at all, going on about the 'quaint charm' of the island and how he simply had to come see where I was 'hiding myself away.'

Each unspoken truth sits heavy in my chest like a held breath before a difficult passage. The magic that now colors my world in shimmers and whispers. Dean's constellations dancing across my skin. The way music has transformed from precise performance into something wild and honest in our lighthouse sanctuary. All these secrets press against my ribs, changing the rhythm of my breathing, altering the melody I've been pretending to play.

Jules gestures with elegant fingers as he describes our upcoming schedule, each movement precise as a conductor's baton. But I'm no longer the instrument I once was, no longer tuned to his particular frequency. I've been restrung by starlight and possibility, my heart keeping time to a different sort of music entirely.

Through the window, autumn leaves dance their subtle magical choreography. If I squint, I can almost see the shimmering wards that protect the island. The same wards that keep Jules from seeing the true Magnolia Cove, just as I've always kept him from seeing my true self.

Dean

The festival grounds are a patchwork of autumn colors and carefully constrained chaos. Vendors arrange displays while magical wards hum beneath my feet—steady, constant, predictable. Unlike the rest of my life lately.

Yesterday, I saw Jules wrap Missy in an enthusiastic hug. She smiled—wide, easy, familiar. It shouldn't have meant anything.

But something in my chest pulled tight and hasn't let go since.

I pop a mint into my mouth as Eleanor and Gerald approach. Gerald licks his lips—a nervous tic he has whenever he must share information someone doesn't want to hear. Judging by the way his gaze darts to me, I'm the unlucky recipient this time.

"About the evening entertainment schedule," Eleanor begins, her voice kind but firm. If there's anyone who isn't afraid to lock horns with me on the council, it's Eleanor Blackwood. "We've had an exciting development."

Gerald nods and licks those lips again. If the world was full of people like him, I'd invest heavily in Chapstick.

"Jules Bouchard has offered to perform," he blurts. "With Margaret Sinclair, of course. Quite a coup for the festival."

He pumps his fist and grins. As if this is a wonderful idea. As if it doesn't risk entirely too much. I gnaw down hard on the mint. "Absolutely not."

"Dean." Eleanor's tone carries decades of handling difficult warlocks. "They're world-class musicians."

"Who happen to be non-magical humans," I bite out. "Or did we forget about maintaining magical security during events? Margaret's effect on magic is unpredictable enough when she plays alone. Add another performer and—"

"Mr. Bouchard was quite insistent." Gerald interrupts, then withers slightly under my glare.

"We are the council that governs this island." My voice carries the edge of steel I've spent years perfecting. "We don't bow to the insistence of visiting musicians."

There's a beat of silence filled with the chatter of vendors setting up their booths, the clatter of decorations being hung, and the hum of last-minute festival preparations.

Eleanor clears her throat and her voice goes soft. "Are you certain that your judgment isn't clouded on this matter?"

The question hits like a physical blow. Behind me, Zoe's laughter carries from the Whimsical Whisk's booth where she's arranging a stand for cupcakes she's labeled 'Autumn Uprising.' The sound grates against my nerves.

Eleanor is right, of course. My judgment is thoroughly, devastatingly clouded. Because I went and fell for someone. Something I'd vowed never to do. And not just anyone—a normal human. A normal human who jumped into another man's arms yesterday without hesitation. Who smiled as she introduced him to her sister, the same sister that I'm pretty certain she still hasn't told about us.

I've spent a decade building walls, maintaining control, protecting the town from exactly these kinds of complications.

Yet here I am, watching all my carefully laid safeguards break because a cellist with autumn-bright eyes and too many questions made me believe, just for a moment, that letting someone in wouldn't end in disaster. But of course it would. Of course it has. Jules Bouchard with his charming smiles and shiny reputation is proof of that—a walking reminder that Missy belongs to a world of spotlight and standing ovations, not hidden magic and small-town secrets.

"We'll need extra security measures," I manage, my voice low and gritty.

"We always do so for festivals," Eleanor says.

I nod sharply and turn away, seeking escape. Thankfully, the booth inspections won't complete themselves. Plus, it gives me something to focus on besides the hollow ache in my chest.

Zoe's wild grin meets me at the Whimsical Whisk's setup. Her purple-streaked hair is twisted into a messy bun, leaving her giant hoop earrings free to sway with every movement. She's perched on the edge of the display table while Ethan arranges their famous pumpkin scones.

"Dean! Just the man we need." She swings her legs. "You like to read, don't you?"

"Read?" It's a surprising enough question that it almost pulls me out of my dark mood. Almost.

Her grin widens, if that's possible and Ethan just huffs a laugh behind her.

"I had this book I loved as a kid," she continues. "This boy drank a fizzy soda, and he almost got diced by the ceiling fan."

Ethan shoots up. "*That's* what you remember from that book?"

She rolls her eyes. "Best scene, boss." She turns back to me. "Anyway, it inspired my Autumn Uprising cupcakes, and I thought—" At this she bats her lashes. As if charm ever works on me. Or as if she's one to bother charming men at all.

Ethan groans. "Please tell me you're not suggesting—"

"Bubbles!" She claps her hands together. "Nothing fancy, just some floating up from bubble machines. But, you know, with a twist."

"A twist," I intone. There's not much I like less in life than a twist.

"When they pop, they're scented. You know, pumpkin spice, maple, maybe a hint of wood smoke..." She places her hands together in a praying motion. "The kids would love it and I'd tell everyone we used essential oils! Pinky swear and hope to die."

Ethan stands to his full height. "The last time you got inspiration from children's literature, you had us handing out lickable wallpaper samples."

"Which were genius." She slams her hand down hard enough that it dislodges a scone. "Not my fault people have no appreciation for innovative dessert delivery systems. But,"—she returns her gaze to me and her eyes widen like a cat begging for a saucer of milk—"who doesn't love bubbles, am I right? And it would barely use any magic at all."

I grit my teeth and hold in a sigh. Ethan meets my gaze and shrugs. The council will, of course, approve mild magic like this—easily explained and designed to deliver the signature wow factor we aim to impress on visitors.

"You'll use standard bubble machines?" I ask.

"Cross my heart and hope my soufflé never rises," she says with such sincerity I can't decide if she's kidding.

"Fine."

"Huzzah!" She jumps up and shakes her hips back and forth in a victory dance. Ethan laughs as he pulls raisin-studded muffins from their case. He's such a perfectionist—he's using the samples to ensure the table looks perfect for the event. He'll pack them up in a few minutes and donate them because that's who Ethan Hart is. The kind of man who remembers everyone on the island's orders, who keeps extra loaves warming for the night shift workers, who built his life around making others happy.

The kind of man Alex fell in love with instantly, without complication.

Something bitter coils in my chest. Ethan's biggest daily crisis is whether the sourdough has the right tang or if the croissants are flaky enough. He gets to use his magic for warmth and comfort and sustenance. Despite being a shifter, he's deeply accepted in the community. The townspeople don't eye him with that mix of respect and wariness they reserve for me.

The weight of my power sits heavy beneath my skin, a constant reminder that my life can never be that uncomplicated. That I can never just be a man who plays guitar and loves freely and doesn't have to worry about whether he'll have to deny a young, powerful witch her life's dream to study outside the island.

A familiar laugh cuts through my spiral. Missy approaches with Alex and Jules, her entire face lit up at something he's said. Her hair catches golden threads of sunlight and her hands paint stories in the air as she talks. Jules leans in close, perfectly timed chuckles punctuating her words.

"And this," Alex says, "is the booth for the Whimsical Whisk. Ethan and Zoe are the geniuses behind it."

Missy meets my gaze, but just as quickly flicks her eyes away. She beams as she makes introductions, her voice carrying the practiced ease of someone who's spent a lifetime charming audiences. As if the last few weeks haven't happened. As if we never shared magic, music, and midnight confessions.

"Dean's our resident killjoy," Zoe announces cheerfully. "But he's what makes the magic happen on the island, so we forgive him."

She winks at me and I struggle not to gape. Zoe's always

cutting things too close. I'll have to speak with her about *that* comment later.

Jules' perfect laugh matches his perfectly coiffed hair. "Ah yes, Missy's already told me about you and your... dedication to the rules."

He extends a hand which I accept. His grip is also infuriatingly perfect—firm enough to convey confidence, brief enough to seem casual, the kind of handshake that opens doors in concert halls and board rooms alike. I withdraw my hand and resist the urge to wipe my palm against my jacket. Of course Missy's been talking about me to him. Probably laughing about the stern council member who takes himself too seriously.

"A pleasure," I grit out. "Speaking of rules, I have other booths to inspect. If you'll excuse me."

I don't wait for a response, just turn and walk away.

"So, Jules," Zoe says as I retreat. "How do you feel about award-winning literature?"

Their laughter trails me. I walk until I reach the gazebo. The nexus point nearby will explain my presence if anyone asks. Not that anyone will. Dean Markham, doing his duty, keeping his distance. Everything as it should be.

"Dean." Missy appears beside me like I've summoned her. "What's wrong?"

"Nothing. Just busy."

She plants her fists on her hips, bracelets clattering with the motion. "You're shutting me out again, so obviously something is wrong."

I nod at Marcus and Mia who walk by with stacks of book crates in their arms. Wait for them to pass. The truth sits bitter on my tongue, sharp as splinters. I could tell Missy that seeing her with Jules felt like watching my reality shatter. How her uninhibited laughter with him exposed every crack in my practiced facade. But vulnerability has never served me well.

"I assume Mr. Bouchard's visit will be brief? We didn't receive any extended stay requests."

"Dean." Her voice has gone whisper-soft. "I know what you saw at the cafe yesterday, but—"

"You don't owe me explanations."

"I don't?" Fire flashes in her eyes. "Explain to me why I don't because I thought this"—she gestures between us—"meant we required explanations."

"Well, maybe you can tell me what this"—I mimic her gestures—"is because you clearly haven't shared with your sister about us and it's left me wondering."

"That's not fair. Jules showed up unexpectedly. I haven't had time—"

"Or maybe you just haven't wanted to."

Her lips part, then close again. "That night in the planetarium changed things for me, Dean. I thought you knew that."

I look at her, then remember the way she hugged Jules yesterday, and something inside me buckles.

"Things change," I say quietly. "Maybe you already have."

The words hang between us, lingering like the last note of a song that leaves your heart aching in silence. Missy's breath catches, and suddenly I can see the hurt beneath her anger. Hurt I've put there, carved from my own fears and planted in soil too fertile for such bitter seeds.

The sunlight emphasizes the gleam in her eyes, the pinch of her lips. When did I become the kind of man who wounds what he means to protect? The kind who takes something as pure and beautiful and joyous as Missy, and taints it with his own darkness.

"I'm sorry." The words feel inadequate, hollow as magic-less ward lines. Behind us, festival preparations continue on with their cheerful cacophony, oblivious to the quiet devastation in our corner of the world. "That was... I shouldn't have said that. This is about me and my insecurities, not you."

Some scars run too deep to heal with simple apologies. I should know—I've spent a decade regretting the ones I gifted my sister. And maybe I've done this on purpose. Maybe I'm pushing Missy away before I can hurt her too. After all, she has another option. Someone whose hands create music instead of magic, whose smile comes easily instead of breaking through years of careful control.

I'd be a fool to not recognize the way Jules looks at her. The way his eyes follow her movements like she's a melody he's trying to memorize.

He'd be a fool *not to* look at her like that. The only actual foolishness here is me letting my feelings get hurt. Missy was summer sunshine. But winter's just around the corner.

She crosses her arms, but her voice softens. "Meet me at the studio tomorrow morning early? Please?"

"Of course."

The agreement slips past my defenses before I can stop it. Maybe because I'm weaker than I pretend. Maybe because endings deserve proper punctuation, even painful ones. Or maybe because some part of me still hopes I'm wrong about all of it—about Jules, about her inevitable departure, about my own capacity for happiness.

Some lies we tell ourselves echo louder in autumn air, when everything beautiful is preparing to fade.

Missy nods, then turns back toward the festival grounds where Jules waits. I watch her walk away and wonder if this is how Nell felt, watching her carefully constructed future crumble. At least Missy won't need memory magic to forget me. Time will do that just fine on its own.

Missy

Stars still pepper the sky as I make my way to Rachel's studio, Giuseppe's familiar weight against my back matching the heaviness in my chest. The autumn air carries a sharp coastal bite that wasn't here yesterday, as if the weather itself is marking how quickly things can change. How a life carefully arranged in familiar patterns can spiral into chaos with one unexpected arrival.

Jules has somehow charmed his way into every corner of my world in less than twenty-four hours—sharing stories over dinner with Alex and Ethan, touring the town with infectious enthusiasm, keeping me up late reviewing his 'improvements' to our compositions.

He's always been like this, demanding attention like a spotlight, leaving no room for shadows or subtle variations. I'd forgotten how exhausting it could be until he swept back into my life, rearranging everything to suit his tempo.

At least his infamous night owl tendencies mean I have these early morning hours to myself. To think. To breathe. To try to untangle the mess I've made of things with Dean.

Yesterday's anger has faded, leaving behind a clearer understanding of what I saw in his eyes at the cafe. The uncertainty. The hurt. He'd told me once, voice low in our lighthouse sanctuary, that he'd never allowed himself to date anyone in Magnolia Cove. His role demanded too much isolation, too much control. And then there was Jules, touching me with the casual possessiveness he's always shown, acting like I was just an extension of his artistic vision—as he always has.

I pull open the studio door, barely setting Giuseppe down before I register Dean's presence. He's wearing his signature black leather jacket, every inch the stern warlock I first met. But when our eyes meet in the pre-dawn light, I see past the walls to the man who gave me music beneath constellations and who sees me for who I really am.

"Dean," I whisper, my voice carrying all the words I haven't said.

He crosses the room and stuffs his hands into his pockets. "Missy, I'm an idiot."

"Yeah, you are."

His body tenses, and I can't help but laugh. He tries to resist, his lips pressing into a firm line, but eventually, a chuckle slips out. The sound warms the space between us as I wrap my arms around his waist.

"I'm sorry," he murmurs into my hair.

"I owe you an apology too." I close my eyes and breathe in the scent of cinnamon and autumn leaves that clings to him, suddenly aware of how right this feels. How the chaos in my mind settles just by being near him. "Jules is... he's a lot. I know how it looked in the cafe, but he's always been like that. Too much, too close, too convinced he knows what's best for everyone. And I'm realizing there's a lot about my past life that doesn't fit anymore."

"Missy—" He protests, but I press my fingers against his lips.

"Let me finish. I've been so caught up in avoiding

confrontation that I've made everything worse. Just give me a few days. Let me get Jules sorted out, and then I'll tell Alex everything. God, I haven't had time to tell her I know about magic yet."

My voice catches as the weight of everything suddenly hits me—all the secrets I've been juggling, the constant guard I've had to keep up, trying to figure out who I am beyond the perfect performer Jules expects me to be. A tear slips down my cheek, then another.

Dean pulls back enough to study my face. His calloused thumbs brush the tears away with a gentleness that makes my heart ache. "Of course," he whispers, fingers lingering against my skin. "Take the time you need. I should have trusted you, trusted this. Instead, I let my... history cloud my judgment." His jaw works for a moment. "I'm not used to having something worth losing." He presses a kiss to my brow.

I lean up and capture his lips with mine. Kissing him is like finding the perfect note in a complicated piece—when everything aligns and you know exactly where you belong. His hands slide into my hair as he deepens the kiss, and for a moment, all the complications fade away. There's just this— his warmth, his touch, the steady beating of his heart against mine.

We settle into our usual morning rhythm, talking about nothing and everything the way we do at the lighthouse. For a moment, everything feels possible again.

Then the door clicks open.

Rachel and Emma enter first. Jules walks in behind them, gesturing with a takeaway cup and smiling that sunshine grin that's landed him on the cover of more than a few magazines. "The Ethiopian beans at this little place in Prague—absolute revelation. Though nothing quite matches the complexity of traditional Indonesian kopi luwak. Have you ever tried it?"

Rachel laughs as she swirls her iced coffee from the Whisk. "I'm afraid my coffee expertise stops at 'better than day-old roast from the Hungry Gull.'"

"Oh darling, we simply must educate your palate!" Jules' eyes sparkle then land on me.

I feel Dean withdraw, physically and emotionally, retreating to his corner as Jules sweeps forward. "Missy! Excellent news—I've managed to negotiate everything despite this charming town's absolutely prehistoric internet service. We can leave next week after all! Vienna is gorgeous this time of year, and don't worry, I've arranged a month off around your sister's wedding. It's all taken care of."

The words slam into me like a wave, knocking me off kilter. Had we vaguely discussed pushing up our timeline in a very theoretical way? Maybe. But I'd dismissed it as Jules being Jules—always planning, always pushing, always ten steps ahead without checking if anyone wants to follow. I hear myself making noncommittal sounds of agreement, falling back into old patterns like muscle memory from too many years of allowing some combination of decision fatigue and conflict avoidance drive me allowing Jules to orchestrate my life.

"Wonderful!" Jules claps his hands together. "Now, let me not monopolize your prodigy's lesson time." He beams at Emma. "Missy has told me all about your extraordinary talent."

Emma blushes furiously, but I barely notice. Because beyond her, Dean's expression has gone completely unguarded for a moment. His mouth is parted, his eyes shimmer, and his fisted hands have gone slack at his sides. It's like watching someone let go of a rope they've clung to. When our gazes meet, his features smooth into granite, cold and impenetrable.

No. No, this is all wrong. He thinks— But I haven't even

discussed leaving early. Jules just assumed, as he always does, that his plans are everyone's plans.

I shift my focus on Emma, trying to calm her nerves as she whispers, "I can't believe Jules Bouchard is watching me play!" But even as I guide and accompany her through the piece, noting how much she's controlling her magic since Dean gave her the necklace, I'm achingly aware of Dean's rigid posture as he stands with Rachel and Jules.

When Emma finishes, Rachel herds her toward the door. Both of them grab bags for school and Jules follows behind. "Oh, Missy. I told Rachel I could go in with her today and meet her other music students. You don't mind, darling, do you?"

"No," I say, before considering how his words might land on Dean's ears. I just want Jules gone. I just want to fix things with Dean. I just want a moment to breathe.

Jules is out the door before I can correct the course, already deep in conversations about the merits of various conservatories. The silence they leave behind feels charged, heavy with all the things I haven't said.

Dean tidies the space with mechanical precision, his movements precise and controlled. Too controlled. My hands fumble as I do a poor job of wiping Giuseppe down. But when Dean heads for the door, I abandon my half-hearted attempt at instrument care and follow him into the light rain, Giuseppe's case banging against my back as leaves swirl in the wind.

He walks so fast I have to jog to keep up. When he stops abruptly, water drips from his hair. "Are you leaving next week? When did you plan to tell me?"

"I haven't agreed to that."

His eyes flash and he pulls a mint from the case in his jacket but doesn't put it in his mouth. "Jules seems convinced."

"Jules hasn't doubted himself since kindergarten. It means nothing."

Dean's shoulders drop. He pinches the bridge of his nose and rain slips down his skin. Then he opens his eyes and sighs. "You need a few days. Take them. But I need to know what we are, Missy. What our future looks like... if we have one." He swallows hard. "Tell me if I've misunderstood things between us. If I have, I'll back off. If I haven't..." His jaw works for a moment. "Then I need to know if leaving early is on the table for you. I can't—" He lets out a rough breath. "I can let people hate me for the greater good. I've spent years doing that. But this?" His gesture encompasses the space between us. "Caring about someone just for myself? I don't know how to do this halfway. I know I'm being intense, but I don't know how else to be, especially when I care about something... or someone."

"You haven't misunderstood," I whisper, but the words feel inadequate against the weight of his honesty. He's willing to go public with me. A regular human. I've barely considered the weight of that decision. He's not just magical, he's a leader. The *head warlock*. And that's probably huge. I wonder if he has to officially note something if he dates someone outside the community. Meanwhile, I can't even decide if I'm staying in town next week. I've been happy to just go with the flow.

The realization slams into me. I've spent years letting others orchestrate my life—Jules with his career plans, our manager with his vision, Alex with her sacrifices. Even now, I'm waiting for someone else to make the hard decisions. But Dean? He orchestrates an entire magical island. Every choice he makes ripples through the lives here. I have to risk telling my sister about us. He has to risk telling an entire magical world that he's chosen me. And here I am, still trying to avoid confrontation, still letting the current carry me wherever it flows easier.

"I'll think through everything, I promise," I whisper into

the cool, rain-kissed air, as mist slowly gathers around us. "Really think it through."

When he kisses me, it's gentle but weighted with everything we've said and haven't said. A wind blows through, beginning another ballet of leaves falling. But for the first time since learning about magic, I can't see its shimmer at all.

Missy

The autumn air shimmers with caramel apples and childhood dreams as we make our way through the Harvest Hoopla. Grammie Rae calls out from the honey candy stand, her voice carrying over the cheerful chaos of carnival games and excited chatter. The scent of pumpkin spice and cinnamon wafts from the Whisk's booth where Ethan and Zoe draw crowds with bubbles that burst and release the warm, cozy aromas. The council, apparently, had taken little convincing to approve that pinch of easily explainable magic.

"You have to try one of these," Alex insists as she pulls me toward her fiancé's booth. "Ethan's been experimenting with the recipe for weeks."

Next thing I know, she's pressing a paper cup with a miniature maple crème brûlée into my hand and giving Ethan a quick kiss before steering us back into the festival crowd and toward our friends again. The dessert's still warm, and wisps of steam curl up from where Ethan's just finished torching the sugar top. The crystallized surface cracks under my spoon. I pop a bite into my mouth and the creamy sweetness has me closing my eyes so I can focus more of my attention on the taste. Which is exactly what Ethan's baking always does. No wonder my sister fell in love with him.

As caramelized sugar dissolves on my tongue, I watch iridescent bubbles floating up from his booth catch the autumn sunlight. Children try to catch them on their tongues and squeal with delight when they burst into puffs of cinnamon-scented air. It's exactly the kind of whimsical touch that makes the Whisk special, though now I understand the magic behind it isn't just metaphorical.

As we reach our group again, I force a smile, trying to match everyone else's festival spirits. But Dean's words from this morning echo in my head. *I don't know how to do this halfway.* The raw honesty in his voice haunts me, making even the twinkling lights and warm laughter feel somewhat bittersweet.

Jules examines a caramel apple with the same critical eye he uses to analyze sheet music. "Quaint," he declares, but his tone suggests he means provincial.

Rachel catches my eye and we share a knowing look. She's been graciously fielding Jules' opinions on everything from the local coffee to the *charming but limited* music program all week. Now she steers us toward the performance area. Emma stands near the front of the stage practically vibrating with energy and clutching her violin case with a death grip.

"Oh my gosh," she says as I walk up to her. "I can't believe I'm actually going to do this."

"You've got this," Rachel says firmly before giving her a hug then heading to find her seat. The rest of the group—even Jules —follow her and take their place, but I linger with Emma another moment. Dean's containment charm glints on the necklace at her throat. The necklace that shouldn't work—technically couldn't work, according to magical theory—but somehow does. Dean had explained it to me, voice low as he admitted bypassing council permission to try his experimental magic.

She deserves a chance, he'd said simply. *Everyone does.*

Looking at Emma now, seeing how her hands have steadied around her violin case, I'm struck by how much he risked helping one young musician follow her dreams. It's so perfectly Dean—gruff exterior hiding a heart that cares almost too much, willing to bend his beloved rules if it means protecting someone who needs it.

"This never would have happened if it wasn't for you, Missy." Emma's eyes shimmer.

"It's been my pleasure." The words come easily because they're true. Even as everything else in my life feels like it's splintering apart, this—helping Emma find her voice through music—feels real. "Here, I have something for you."

My hands tremble as I pull out the envelope. Emma accepts then her eyes widen as she reads the contents.

"Wait, is this..."

"A copy of my letter of recommendation for Juilliard that I'm ready to submit whenever you put in your application next year."

Before I can think, she launches herself at me in a fierce hug that nearly knocks us both over. As I hold her, I realize that even if everything else is falling apart, I've done this one good thing. I've helped someone else's dream take flight, even as my own hopes feel increasingly uncertain.

"I mean every one of those words," I whisper into Emma's curls. "Remember them when you're playing."

Emma gives me another squeeze, wipes her cheeks, and clutches her violin case to herself before walking toward the stairs. Finding my seat beside Alex, I try to push away the gnawing questions. What am I besides a cellist? I've spent my entire life becoming one specific thing—would I even know how to be anything else? The thought of trying to build a life here, of being something other than the person I've trained to be since I was twelve, terrifies me in a way I can't quite articulate.

My heart, more and more, wants to stay in this magical place where the pecan pie tastes like snuggling under a blanket on a rainy day and the friendship feels like coming home again. Where Dean's rare smiles feel more valuable than any standing ovation. But what is here for me, really?

I don't have a teaching certificate, and besides, Rachel is already the music teacher at the local school. Private lessons could never support me full-time in a town this small. I can barely make grilled cheese without setting off the smoke alarm —it's always been takeout and room service between performances since I stopped living with Alex. I've put every waking moment since middle school into becoming Margaret Sinclair, world-renowned cellist. And that woman doesn't belong in Magnolia Cove.

Alex nudges my shoulder. "Remember your Juilliard audition? I was so nervous I almost threw up in Mom's favorite houseplant."

"You were always more nervous than I was at my performances." I laugh, the memory warming something inside me. "Remember how you used to squeeze Dad's hand so hard during my solos that he'd pretend they'd gone numb the rest of the night?"

Alex grins. "Someone had to be nervous! You were always so composed, even back then."

The familiar banter settles something in my chest. We've stayed close despite the distance, despite my hectic touring schedule. Maybe... maybe other relationships could survive as well. But the thought slips away as Emma takes the stage.

Her performance is flawless. I hold my breath as I watch. It seems the council members do too, but not a whisper of magic escapes. Her music flows true, exactly as we practiced.

Dean stands tucked into the back corner of the stage, a

shadow in his black leather jacket. Not long ago, I would have read his stance as intimidating, his presence as just another example of his need to control everything. Now I see the way his shoulders carry the weight of protection, how his focus remains on Emma, ready to intervene should her magic spiral. He's positioned himself perfectly—close enough to help if needed, but far enough that Emma won't feel watched or pressured.

My heart does that familiar flutter when his gaze briefly meets mine. Even across the distance, that connection zings between us like a perfectly tuned string. I want to go to him, to feel his arms around me, to lose myself in one of those kisses that make the world fade away except for the hum of magic in the air.

He shifts slightly, adjusts his stance, and I have to bite back a smile. Because I see past the cranky council member and the biting two-word responses. He still moves like he's carrying the weight of the world, still trying to protect everyone. It's no wonder I fell for him so hard.

Emma draws her bow across the strings in a perfect crescendo, her eyes closed in concentration, completely lost in the music. Just watching her, I can feel every hour of practice, every small victory, every breakthrough we've shared coming together at this moment. Pride swells in my chest as she takes her bow to enthusiastic applause.

I gather my empty cup, intending to find Dean—to try to explain the mess of emotions I haven't quite sorted out myself —but Jules materializes in front of me.

"Your prodigy does her teacher justice." He beams that herculean smile he loves to wield.

"Thanks, Jules."

His eyes twinkle in the setting sun and I understand how his charm is so easy to fall for, when those emerald eyes glisten under stage light and he looks at you like you're the only melody worth listening to. It's the same charm that's carried him through three albums and countless performances, that makes audiences lean forward in their seats. But now it feels like a familiar song I've heard too many times—all technical perfection with no real heart behind it.

"So, this evening after our performance, we'll work on the album?" he asks. "When will you be done here?"

"I'm enjoying the Hoopla today, Jules, we've discussed this."

His smile tightens. "You keep giving one excuse after another. I'm only here for a couple more days. When else are we going to work on it?"

He's right, of course. We do need to finish the album. I'm being unprofessional, disappointing our label, our fans, our manager. And him. Just because maybe I don't want this career anymore, doesn't mean Jules doesn't. He's yoked his career to mine and I'm letting him down. "I'm sorry, Jules. I'm distracted."

He shrugs. "It's this town—charming as it may be. It's thrown off your focus. You remember I told you it would."

"You did." I struggle to keep the words from sounding bitter.

He pulls an envelope from his jacket—crisp white paper with my name in his precise handwriting. "I've printed the contract for you. We need to make this official if we're going to keep our performance slots."

The weight of the envelope feels like lead in my hands. Everything I've worked for, everything I've been, condensed into legal terminology and touring dates. It should feel familiar. Instead, it feels like chains.

"I'll get my parts done," I promise, but even I can hear the lack of conviction in my voice.

Jules leaves with the explanation that he vowed to take a picture with the young star performer, leaving me clutching the envelope and trying not to think about our upcoming performance. How are we supposed to harmonize when everything feels so discordant?

Alex appears at my elbow, her brow furrowed. "Hey, sis. Can I get you a cup of tea before your show?"

"Sure."

We end up at a food truck getting a Harvest Moon Chai—cinnamon and cardamom and that pinch of magic that feels like comfort. Like Magnolia Cove itself. Which only makes everything harder.

Alex leads us to a picnic table beneath an ancient oak tree where Spanish moss hangs down like a curtain, creating an illusion of privacy. I set the envelope on the table, Jules' handwriting staring up at me like an accusation.

"Everything okay?" Alex asks softly.

I paste on my performer's smile, the one that's gotten me through countless uncomfortable donor meetings and less-than-perfect venues. "Looks like I'm going touring again!" I wave the envelope with forced cheerfulness. "Don't worry, I'll be back the month before the wedding. I wouldn't miss it for anything."

Alex's eyes narrow. She's quiet for a beat, her pink painted fingernails gripping her paper teacup so tightly she leaves dents in its side. Finally she releases a breath. "Okay, I know you're an adult and maybe it's not my place, but I can't take it another minute. Missy, what's wrong?"

Something in her gentle tone breaks me. My hands shake around my cooling cup and suddenly I'm crying—ugly tears that do not belong at a public festival. No, they belong firmly in one's private bedroom. Preferably in a house. With no neighbors.

"Oh, Missy." Alex pulls me into a fierce hug that reminds me of skinned knees and first heartbreaks, of all the times she's been my shelter from the storm.

When I can finally breathe again, I whisper, "There's something I need to tell you."

"Anything. Always." She brushes a bit of hair back from my face.

"I know about magic."

She stills for a moment, then lets out a long breath. "Oh, good. That's a relief. I've hated keeping the secret from you."

"I understand why you've had to, though." I twist my hands in my lap. "But there's something else too." Deep breath. "I've been seeing Dean Markham... like romantically."

The silence stretches so long I finally force myself to look up. To my complete surprise, Alex is grinning.

"Did you hear what I said?"

"Missy, half the island knows that."

"What!?" Heat floods my cheeks. "We've told no one."

"It's a small town. And you two can't be within a hundred feet of each other without gravitating together like magnets. Dean's been at the cafe more in the past month than in the entire time I've lived here and he's visiting the Whisk more frequently as well. And I doubt it's to hear Zoe's latest and increasingly dramatic wedding cake ideas she regales him with every time he stops in. Plus, you get a little smile every time someone mentions his name—like you're doing right now."

My face burns hotter. "Are you... are you mad at me?"

She grabs my hand and squeezes it fiercely. "No, Missy. No, of course not. I mean Dean is... well... he's Dean." She pauses and takes a considering sip of her tea. "I've never thought he was a bad guy, though, just... intense?"

"He just cares so much... about Magnolia Cove and protecting it." The words come out soft, almost defensive.

Alex's eyebrows lift but she clutches her hands around her tea like she's warming her fingers and pauses for a moment before speaking. "And what about you? How do you feel?"

"Honestly?"

"Completely." She smiles.

I return it but my voice is shaky. "Terrified that I'm letting everyone down." The words tumble out like they've waited for their chance to escape. "That I'll mess things up for you by dating the Head Warlock of the town you love, and I'm letting Jules down by not getting work for the album done, and I'm letting my manager down by not committing, and—"

"Missy." Alex places a hand on my arm like she's pausing me. "You have never let me down. I've always wanted you to be happy. If a cranky warlock achieves that, then I can support it."

A laugh bubbles up unexpectedly. "Oh my gosh, he's so cranky, isn't he?"

"Very." Alex chuckles, then her expression softens. "It sounds like you're focused on everyone else, but what do you want? If you owed no one else anything, what would you do?"

The questions slam into me. I open my mouth, but nothing comes out. It's such a simple question—what do I want?—but I realize I've spent so long trying to live up to everyone else's expectations I'm not sure I know the answer.

"I don't know," I finally whisper.

"How about stop worrying about the rest of us, and figure out the answer to that? Hmm?"

I pull her into another hug, breathing in the familiar scent of vanilla and spices. The scents of the bakery and cafe. Of her and Ethan's home. "I need to warm up before the performance."

"I'll be in the front row, cheering you on like always." She squeezes my hand, then a mischievous glint enters her eye. "And I need to go track down my fiancé and tease him relentlessly. He lost our bet."

"Your bet?"

"Mhmm. I bet him a week of shoulder rubs that you and Dean were seeing each other. He said not a chance."

"Wait, why did he think there wasn't a chance?"

"Mostly because Ethan would rather imagine a world where sugar disappears than one that involved dating Dean Markham." She places a quick kiss on my cheek. "But he also doesn't like flavored coffees, so take his opinion with a grain of salt."

Her words pull another laugh from me, one that fades as she heads back into the festival. She weaves through the crowd, stopping to chat with what seems like everyone she passes. She belongs here completely—the food writer who found her authentic story, the sister who finally got to build her own life instead of just supporting mine.

Alex glances back over her shoulder with a wicked grin. "Oh, and while we're spilling secrets—just in case Dean hasn't told you yet—Ethan's a shifter. Okay love you, bye!"

She disappears into the crowd, leaving me blinking after her like she just told me the sky was lime-green. I sit there for a beat, absorbing it. Okay... that's shocking. But also... fine. Ethan is a great guy. A steady presence. That doesn't change because he's a shifter. Though I definitely need more details about what, exactly, that entails.

The sound of the Harvest Hoopla drifts over—children's laughter, carnival music, the constant hum of happiness and community. From my seat beneath the oak tree, it all feels like a snow globe scene, one I'm watching from the outside. Alex has her cafe and Ethan and friends that feel like family, Emma has her music and magic, even Jules knows exactly who he is and what he wants. But me?

I'm sitting on a bench beneath a tree as old as some of the music I play, clutching a contract for a life I'm not sure I want anymore. Afraid to reach for something different, something real. Maybe I've spent so many years moving from stage to stage, city to city, that I don't know how to be anything but temporary.

Dean

Twilight bleeds across the festival grounds, painting everything in shades of uncertainty. I stand at the back of the crowd, far enough that no one notices me but close enough to intervene if needed. Not that I should be here at all. Eleanor's perfectly capable of handling any magical disruptions. More capable, probably, given how compromised I am.

The thought sits bitter on my tongue as Missy takes the stage with Giuseppe. Even in the fading light, she glows. Her movements are precise, practiced—exactly what you'd expect from a world-class musician. Jules joins her, their instruments weaving together a song in intricate patterns that leave the crowd breathless.

It should be beautiful. It is beautiful, in the way cut crystal is beautiful—pristine, perfect, hollow.

I've seen Missy play differently. Wrapped in starlight and blankets at the lighthouse, her eyes closed, her soul bare. Playing not because she should, but because the music lived in her bones and demanded release. The performance is nothing like that. This is craft without heart, technique without truth.

The magic responds anyway. Of course it does. The wards

strengthen with each note, humming in harmony with her music like they always do. Like they shouldn't. It eats at me—the lack of explanation.

Missy's eyes remain fixed on some distant point, never meeting the audience. It's like she's not really here at all. When I'd imagined her taking the stage, it was nothing like this. I'd envisioned her as she was twirling in circles beneath my magic in the planetarium. Alive and vivid. Instead, she seems like a husk. My fingers itch to halt the performance, to stride onto that stage and break whatever invisible chains bind her to this pristine prison of perfection. But I have no right. No reason. The magic flows smooth and strong, and my own selfish concerns aren't grounds for intervention.

When they finally finish, relief floods through me like high tide. Emma rushes forward to hug Missy, and despite everything, I smile. This is the Missy I know—the one who nurtures young talent, who sees past Emma's struggles to her potential. The one who might leave next week without warning, taking her light and her music and leaving me with memories that won't be enough.

I turn away, pushing through the crowd toward the nexus point. The wards need checking with so many humans present, even if Missy's music has somehow stabilized them again. Another mystery I'll never solve if—

"Wearing your extra-grumpy-council-member face today?"

Her voice stops me like a spell. When I turn, starlight catches in her hair, and for a moment, I forget every reason I shouldn't reach for her. I tuck my hands into my pockets instead. "We all have our roles to play."

Something flickers across her face—pain, maybe—before her expression clears. "Really? What's mine?"

Beauty. Grace. Joy. The woman who makes my magic stronger and my walls weaker. The normal human who somehow sees too much and feels too deeply. The one I'm fool enough to love.

I shrug, swallowing truth for safer words. "Somebody has to be the favorite."

She scrunches her nose. "Jules has already taken that spot and anchored himself onto it. I'll need something else."

I drift closer, pulled into her orbit as always. "No desire to steal the spotlight from him?" She could take it if she wanted. Jules is brilliant, polished, perfect. But Missy has something wild and untamed that even she doesn't seem to fully understand. Jules may have mastered every technical aspect of the performance, but he'll never have what Missy has. That spark that makes magic itself lean in to listen.

She only smirks, though. "I wish I could chuck it at him and knock that charming smile off his face." A laugh escapes me before I can stop it. "But no," she says softer. "No desire for that, I don't think."

"Well, then..." My fingers flex in my pockets, fighting the urge to touch her. The festival lights paint her skin in amber and gold, making her look like a fairy in a children's book, beckoning humans to wander into her enchanted ring and never leave. "Perhaps your role could be the woman who trips over council members when she visits new towns?"

"Hey!" Her laughter rings into the cooling air, genuine and warm in a way her performance smile never is. The sound draws me closer, like magic responding to her music. Like a moth to flame. Like a fool to fate.

"Or woman who doesn't pay attention to weather reports?"

"That was an accident!" Her hand lands on my arm, and warmth spreads through me like summer sun. Her touch burns through my jacket's leather, through my carefully constructed walls, through every reason I've given myself why this can't work.

The festival fades around us. The nexus point I'm supposed to be checking, the wards I maintain, the duties I've built my life around, all of it recedes until there's just this. Just her eyes catching starlight, her fingers grazing my bicep, the way she sways slightly closer as if she can't help herself either.

I should step back. Should remember I'm the Head Warlock, should maintain appropriate distance. Instead, I find myself fixed on the curve of her smile, the glimmer of her lips.

"I seem to recall," I say, voice dropping lower, "that you're the one who chose to practice in a storm."

She tilts her head, and god help me, but I want to brush back that strand of hair falling across her cheek. "If I knew who would rescue me—and what that night would lead to—I'd do it again."

The certainty in her voice undoes me. This is how we keep happening—these small moments that feel bigger than magic, these quiet conversations that make me forget why I've spent years keeping everyone at an arm's length.

"Dean?"

The voice hits like ice water, snapping me to attention. I whip around to find my mother standing before us, my father beside her. Both are staring at us with mouths agape and brows furrowed. Both staring at Missy's hand on my arm. At how close we're standing. At what they must recognize as history preparing to repeat itself. Because they'll know she's non-magical. She has no aura at all.

They're not the only ones staring, either. Grammie Rae watches from her booth, wearing that knowing smirk that makes me want to add sound-blocking wards around her house out of spite. Others are trying to appear like they're not looking our way. We might as well have been dancing in the street.

"Mom?" The word scrapes my throat.

Missy takes a step back from me and produces that perfect

performer's smile that never reaches her eyes. "Oh, hello, I'm Missy."

She extends her hand. They stare at it like she's offering them poison. After an incredibly awkward moment where even the festival itself seems to have gone quiet, she withdraws and wipes her palm against her blouse. A shaky laugh spills from her as she speaks. "I'll excuse myself. See you later, Dean."

"Missy, wait—" I reach for her, but she's already gone, swallowed by the festival crowd.

My parents' stares weigh like stones.

"I just need to check over the wards once more," I manage. "Let me finish up and we can go to my house."

The ocean's roar almost drowns my thoughts as I watch my father examine my bookshelves without seeing them, one hand pressed against his mouth. Mother's quiet sniffling from the kitchen table makes everything worse.

"Dean," she starts, voice trembling, "was that young woman... was she... I mean is she..."

"Yes, Mom. She's non-magical."

Fresh tears spill down her cheeks. My father drops his hand. "Dean. Son." He shakes his head slowly. "We love you, and we're so proud of everything you've done here in Magnolia Cove, but a non-magical woman, son? Is she even connected to the community?"

I suck a breath in over my teeth. My fingers itch to reach for a mint, but I refuse to show that tell. Not now. Not during this conversation that shouldn't even be happening. "Only through her sister who is marrying a local."

"She's marrying a witch or a warlock?"

"No."

The question grates against my nerves. As if he doesn't already know. As if thirty-five years on the National Council hasn't taught him exactly how rare—how impossible—these connections are. He's watched enough powerful magic users fall from grace over human entanglements to fill a library of cautionary tales. And here I am, Head Warlock of Magnolia Cove somehow following the same worn path to ruin.

His disappointment settles around my shoulders like a cloak. Council members don't fraternize with non-magical people. We definitely don't fall in love with them. These are the rules that have kept our world safe, our magic protected. Rules I helped write. Rules I'm breaking every time I let Missy slip past my defenses.

"We came here"—Mom chokes out—"to try to convince you to come to Nell's wedding only to find you repeating the same choices that tore our family apart."

"We supported Nell too, remember?" Dad's laugh holds no humor. "Thought we were being progressive. Had her boyfriend over for Sunday dinners."

Mom nods and dabs at her eyes. "And look where that got us. Ten years of barely seeing our son. A decade for our daughter to heal from the scars it left."

"I know well that's my fault." A headache builds in my temple, causing the vein there to throb. Old guilt rises like high tide, familiar as magic, bitter as mint-flavored regret. Ten years of carefully maintained distance, of watching my family fracture like ward lines under too much pressure. Of being the one who made the hard choice, who did what needed to be done, who chose duty over love.

I flex my fingers, fighting the urge to reinforce the wards around the cottage—my knee-jerk reaction to any turbulence. As if magical barriers could protect any of us from the consequences of our choices. As if they ever had.

My parents both blink at me. Dad's face softens some. "We don't blame you, Dean."

"You don't have to. I blame myself." I take a breath only to realize that I've unconsciously reached for memory magic, my power responding to the memories too intently. The taste of mint—sharp and cold like the first frost of winter—fills my mouth. "I know how much I hurt Nell. Why do you think I'm not planning to attend her wedding? Because I'm selfish? Because I don't care?" My laugh comes out rough as sea spray. "It's because I won't risk casting shadows on the day she deserves nothing but light."

My father frowns. "She wants you there, son."

"She hasn't told me that."

Mom crumples her tissue. "You're both too stubborn. Always have been."

"At the moment,"—Dad cuts in—"that's not the most pressing issue." His voice hardens. "This woman—this Missy —someone without magic, Dean? You, of anyone, know that people like us can't date normal humans. We thought you'd have learned that from everything that happened with Nell."

"I did." I pinch the bridge of my nose. "I mean, I have. Missy is different."

Mom rises. "How? How is she different?"

The words I plan to speak die in my throat. Because Missy is probably leaving next week. Because I've turned her into a security risk by showing her our world. Because my heart says she's different, but my heart's an idiot that should have learned its lesson a decade ago.

The ocean's rhythmic rush fills the silence, steady as a heart-beat, relentless as guilt. A decade of carefully maintained control threatens to crumble beneath the weight of their expectations, their fears, their love. The same love that made them welcome Charlie to Sunday dinners, that made them believe in second chances, that made the eventual fallout cut so much deeper. Some patterns repeat like tides against the shore, wearing away at resolve until nothing remains but bare rock and bitter truth.

"If it means so much to you, I'll attend the wedding." After all, I've had a decade to perfect the art of staying on the edges. I can keep to the shadows, nod at the right times, and slip away before anyone notices.

Mom cries again. Dad closes the space between us and settles a heavy hand on my shoulder. "I knew you'd do the right thing, son. You always do."

His eyes bore into me, dark and knowing as storm clouds. The weight of unspoken meaning hangs between us—because this isn't just about Nell's wedding. This is about Missy. About duty. About the choices a Head Warlock must make to protect his community. About how some patterns shouldn't be repeated, no matter what the heart says.

The praise settles like chains around my shoulders. Always doing the right thing. Always protecting everyone else. Always sacrificing what I want for what needs to be done.

The ocean's roar fills my cottage, making my headache throb even more intensely. Outside, waves crash against the shore—relentless, inevitable, wearing away at stone until nothing remains but sand and salt and surrender.

Missy

Dawn makes the lighthouse's pale surface appear coral and gritty, like a seashell from the beach. The waves below keep perfect time like a metronome counting down moments I don't want to face. Seabirds wheel through the morning mist, their cries sound mournful without my cello to answer.

It feels wrong to be here without Giuseppe. Like showing up to karaoke without a voice. But maybe that's fitting—I'm not here to make music. I'm afraid I'm here to say goodbye.

The contract in my pocket weighs like lead, Jules' elegant handwriting mapping out a future I can't fight. But Dean's parents' faces haunt me more than any touring schedule. I've spent the night replaying their expressions—the shimmering eyes of his mother, the gaping mouth of his father. The way they looked at me like I was a dissonant note that could shatter their carefully maintained harmony.

I understand family disappointment. I've spent years trying to be worth Alex's sacrifices. But this feels different. Deeper. Like I'm not just disappointing them, but threatening their entire world. Maybe it's the non-magical thing. Or maybe... my throat tightens as I remember Dean mentioning

155

his sister's upcoming wedding. Maybe the idea of him settling here, with me, is what truly devastated them.

A twig snaps behind me and my heart lurches. Dean emerges from the forest path, and just the sight of him makes my chest ache. He's wearing a black button-down with the sleeves rolled up. No jacket. It's like he's peeled off his armor, but somehow it doesn't feel like a hopeful gesture. The shadows under his eyes match the stubble on his jaw. He looks like he's slept about as much as I have.

My heart screams that I'm the last thing he should worry about. He has an entire magical community to protect. His family to reconcile with. His sister's wedding to consider. But when his eyes meet mine, that rare genuine smile breaks across his face, softening the hard lines and wrinkling his eyes.

I cross to him. He seems hesitant to touch me so I wrap my arms around his waist. With a sigh, he pulls me closer. He smells like autumn itself— something distinctly magical that I've come to associate with his presence. If food in Magnolia Cove can taste like comfort, I've decided Dean's smell is safety. But it's not from any magical enhancement. That's just who he is. Which only makes this harder, because I already knew it wouldn't be simple.

Magic and music, duty and dreams—we were always going to be a complicated melody. But this is different. The memory of his mother's horror-stricken face cuts through me. I lost my parents young enough that their absences have become a familiar ache. Alex is all the family I have left, and she gave up so much to make sure I never felt alone. How can I ask Dean to risk his chance at healing his own family? To choose me over bridging the decade-wide gap with his sister, over mending what's broken with his parents?

I can't.

I won't

Because another thing Alex taught me was love. Real love

isn't about perfect harmony or flawless performances. It's about knowing when to step back, when to let the music breathe, when to give someone else the solo. It's about recognizing that sometimes the most profound way to care for someone is to become a rest in their melody rather than trying to force yourself into their score.

And right now, loving Dean means giving him the space to reconcile with his family, to mend what's broken, to find his way back to the people who knew his heart before I ever did. Even if it means my heart breaks in the process.

"I'm sorry about my parents' reaction," he says into my hair.

I curl my fingers around his hips. Everything in me wants to hold on to him forever. "It's okay. It's not a big—"

"It is." He pushes back slightly so he can cup my cheek with his hand. "They're just acting out of fear."

The tenderness in his touch makes my throat tight. This feels simultaneously so right and so wrong. When he kisses me, it's soft and slow and I'm too busy trying to memorize it to actually enjoy it.

I force myself to let him go. To take a step back. "Their fears aren't unfounded though."

He frowns. "What do you mean?"

"You're the Head Warlock of a magical island, Dean." I raise my arms out like I can encompass all of Magnolia Cove. Of everything he protects. "And I'm a woman who barely read fairytales as a kid, much less grew up with any magic, and I'm about to leave."

Because I've realized leaving fixes everything. I can't earn a real living here. Not the kind I need to survive. Staying means stepping in where I don't belong—distracting Alex from the life she's finally building and distracting Dean from the family he's still trying to save. If I go, maybe they'll both be able to breathe easier. Maybe I will too.

Pain flashes across his face, quick as lightning but just as intense. He masters it almost immediately, but I've learned to read the weight in his pauses.

"We can make it work." His voice carries the desperate edge of someone trying to hold on to smoke. "Long distance isn't impossible. I could visit during my vacation time and you'll be in Magnolia Cove to see your sister anyway and—"

A whimper escapes before I can catch it, because god, that's exactly what I wanted to hear. What I'd dared to hope for in the darkest hours of last night. But hope is a cruel companion when reality has other plans.

"Look me in the eye," I whisper, "and tell me your parents will accept you dating me."

The silence stretches between us like a string pulled too tight, trembling on the verge of breaking, its tension humming in the air.

When I part my lips again, I'm still whispering. "Tell me that dating me wouldn't further harm your relationship with them."

He huffs a breath and pinches the bridge of his nose. "My relationship with my parents has always been complicated and—"

"—and you love them."

"Of course I do, but Missy, I love—"

"If you choose me and it fractures your family more, you'll live to regret it." The lump in my throat feels impossible to speak past. It took everything in me to cut him off, to not let him finish what he was about to say. "Take it from someone who doesn't have her parents around to work things out with anymore."

"What about what I want?" He claps a hand to his chest. There's a desperate edge to his voice now. "I was up all night and I've thought through things. I'll work it out with my parents. If they can't accept us, that's on them."

I walk closer to him again. Golden leaves spiral down around us. The trees are almost bare now, stripped down to their essence like this moment is stripping us down to ours.

"Dean," I breathe as I take his hand. "Take it from someone who followed her passion right to misery and obligation." I run my thumb over his fingers, along his wrist, memorizing the warmth I'm choosing to let go. "I feel about you—" The words catch in my throat because they're too big, too real to say out loud. "God, Dean, I care about you more than I've let myself care about anything that wasn't my sister or my cello basically ever. But this burning we feel now..." I press my hand against his chest where I can feel his heartbeat, steady as a metronome. "If we let it consume everything around you, if it burns bridges you might never rebuild... then I could never live with that."

The haunted expression that crosses his face nearly breaks my resolve. But I've seen that same look in old photos of Alex, in the moments when she thought I wasn't watching—the weight of choosing between what you want and what you know is right.

I'd stayed up late with Alex and Ethan, nursing cups of Comforting Chamomile that grew cold as they answered my questions about Dean's family and obligations. About just how much Dean stands to lose.

His parents aren't just any council members—they're part of the national magical governing body, an influence that shapes entire communities. This isn't just about family dinners and holiday gatherings, though that alone would be enough to make me step back.

But no, this is about Dean's entire future, about the delicate balance of power and trust he's spent years building. The realization sits heavy in my chest. My presence in his life would not only strain family bonds, it could unravel the very fabric of his carefully constructed world. And just like Alex chose my future over her own dreams all those years ago, I have to choose Dean's future over my selfish desire to be part of it.

Truth settles like an early winter frost. My career needs me and Dean's family and this community need him. Jules staked his future on mine. Our fans are waiting, our manager's calling, and there are contracts I've already signed. I can't just vanish into a town most people don't even know exists. Maybe Dean and I were foolish to pursue whatever this was between us. A fall fling? Is that even a thing? God, I didn't even do a fling right. But even thinking that word makes me want to sob, because I know Dean is more than a passing infatuation.

Something in Dean's eyes breaks my heart all over again. "Missy, listen to me, I—"

"Don't." I cut him off before he can say whatever wonderful, terrible thing is trying to escape. "Just because a melody is beautiful, doesn't mean you can capture it forever."

He grits his teeth. "People do that all the time. Everyone records music. You're preparing to record an album right now."

I sigh but force myself to keep his gaze. "And do the recordings have the same magic as hearing someone play the same song live?"

He freezes, the way autumn leaves still when the wind suddenly dies. For a long moment, the only movement is the subtle shift of magic in the surrounding air. In his eyes, understanding dawns. He knows I'm not backing down. His shoulders settle into a resignation that breaks my heart more thoroughly than any anger could have.

Because this is Dean—my impossible warlock who bends rules to protect young musicians' dreams but stands rigid in defense of his community. Who tastes like autumn winds and laughs like the ocean crashing against shore. Who makes magic sing in harmony with my music in ways I'll never fully understand. And he knows, just as I do, that some songs are ephemeral. That their beauty lies precisely in their temporary nature, knowing that they exist only in that perfect moment before the world changes key.

"I have one request."

Dean nods without his shoulders loosening. His brow has bunched into a riot of wrinkles. I want to hug him so badly. Or tease him. Or tell him I love him too. Foolishly. Enough to keep me from selfishly pursuing my happiness but potentially ruining his.

"May I keep the knowledge of magic?" The words spill loose and wildly from me. "It lets me actually know about Alex's world and I'll keep the secret, I promise."

Something shimmers in his eyes—maybe magic, maybe tears—before he answers gruffly. "Of course you can."

"Thank you." The whisper barely carries over the waves' roar. Another silence stretches between us, filled with all the things we aren't saying. "So, I guess this is it, then?"

He swallows hard and turns his face away where I can't see it. When he lifts his face again, the expression is completely gone. "Unless you'd like to trip over me again? For old times' sake?" He smiles, but it's forced.

I release a shaky laugh that's fifty percent nerves and fifty percent an attempt to not cry. "Would that result in me getting a lecture from a grumpy warlock in his office?"

His smile softens into something more genuine, though the sadness lingers in his eyes. "I'm afraid you'd have to settle for a slightly less grumpy warlock these days. Someone's been a terrible influence on my carefully cultivated scowl."

"It's comforting to know I've done at least some good during my visit."

"More than you know."

His voice carries a depth that makes my chest ache— because I understand exactly what he means. I want to tell him he's done the same for me. That he's shown me how to find magic in ordinary moments, that he's helped me rediscover what music felt like before it became weighted with expectations and obligations. How his carefully maintained control made every genuine smile, every unguarded moment, feel like discovering a rare pearl.

But speaking that aloud would only make this harder for both of us. I force myself to smile. "Try not to be too cranky with the tourists without me."

"I make no promises." He reaches out like he might brush his knuckles over my cheeks, then lets his hand fall. "Goodbye, Missy."

I turn away before I can change my mind, before I let my traitorous heart choose my happiness over his well-being. The rising sun paints everything in shades of gold and it feels cruel. Wrong. Why isn't rain falling now? Why isn't the world crying the tears I'm fighting?

Behind me, I swear I hear him whisper something that sounds like 'I love you,' but it might just be the wind rattling the remaining leaves, carrying away the last notes of a song we never got to finish.

Missy

The kitchen counter has disappeared beneath a sea of mixing bowls, Alex and I falling into our old habits from the cramped apartment we once shared. It's probably good Ethan's at work —his methodical nature would surely twitch at the disorder we've created.

Ella Fitzgerald's voice drifts from the record player, smooth as silk and infinitely more graceful than the chaos in my head. The steady patter of rain against the windowpanes makes the cottage feel like a warm sanctuary, all cinnamon-scented and glowing from within. The kettle lets out a soft whistle from the stove, promising another cup of the spiced chai Alex has brewed all morning, making the entire house smell like comfort.

"A little to the left," Alex suggests, tilting her head to look at my cracker arrangement. She's perched on a barstool, carefully cutting a block of cheddar into perfect triangles. Her wedding planning binder sits closed on the counter, its pages bristling with sticky notes in a rainbow of colors. "Last book club I made a cracker tower to go with the book." She laughs and rolls her eyes. "It was this ridiculous romance Tom and Rhianna loved about a werewolf princess asleep in a tower."

I stifle a laugh. "How did you get roped into reading that one?"

She snorts as she arranges a pile of grapes. "You'd be amazed what you can get roped into in Magnolia Cove."

I wouldn't, though. After my season with Dean, nothing about this magical town could surprise me anymore. Not the way sunrise catches in the air like possibility, how music resonates differently here, not even how loving someone could feel simultaneously like coming home and leaving it.

Alex hands me another mug of tea. I take a drink but the smell hits. Autumn leaves softened by cinnamon. With trembling hands, I place the mug down and try not to remember who smells like that. I focus on arranging another row of crackers, trying to lose myself in the precise geometry of the task like I've spent the last few days losing myself in recording the album with Jules.

But Jules' music feels hollow now, each note perfectly placed but lacking something essential. I've spent endless hours in Rachel's studio, trying to breathe life into arrangements that once would have thrilled me with their technical brilliance. Now they feel like architectural sketches of emotion rather than the real thing—beautiful outlines of feeling without the messy, vital pulse of actual life beneath them.

Jules composes like a mathematician mapping a complicated formula. Before Dean, I would have called it masterful. Now I understand the difference between precision and truth, between playing the right notes and playing the ones that matter.

I move on to a stack of chocolate chip cookies waiting to be artfully scattered across the board. Their sweet scent mingles with the tea's spicy blend.

The quiet between us feels comforting, wrapped in Ella Fitzgerald's crooning and morning light. Alex hums along, slightly off-key and utterly unselfconscious. I think about Ethan and Alex's morning routine—how they're both disgustingly cheerful before six AM, how they dance around each other in the kitchen.

Really, I'm trying to think about anything but Dean. Anything but his face at the lighthouse. Or how his voice caught when he tried to argue. How doing the right thing feels an awful lot like taking a hammer to my heart.

"You've been working really hard this week," Alex says, her voice gentle in a way that means she sees right through me.

"Uh, yeah, I know. We're trying to record this album before Jules leaves."

She hums a reply as she continues slicing the cheese. "Have you had a chance to see Dean?"

The cookie slips from my fingers, landing with a soft thud that echoes the way my heart keeps dropping whenever I hear his name. The tears come before I can stop them—hot and insistent and mortifying. They've been doing this all week, ambushing me in moments when I least expect it: during rehearsals when the magic doesn't sing beneath the notes, in the Hungry Gull cafe when I catch a whiff of autumn spice, or in the dead of night when I can't decide if I made the right choice.

Alex drops her knife with a clatter and wraps her arms around me, pulling me tight against her shoulder. She smells like home. The tears come faster now, hot and insistent against her soft sweater.

"I ended things with Dean," I whisper, the words falling like broken notes into the quiet kitchen. "I mean, I have a career that takes me across oceans. He's the Head Warlock of a magical island which is a job with a lot of pressure. It was never going to..." My voice catches, remembering the way twinkle lights caught in his eyes at the lighthouse, how even his silence felt like a song I wanted to learn by heart. "It just wasn't going to work."

"Oh, Missy." Alex's arms tighten, and for a moment I'm transported back to every heartbreak she's held me through—failed auditions, lost scholarships, the days we buried our parents. But this feels different. Those were wounds inflicted by fate or circumstances. This time, I'm the one wielding the knife.

"I'm sorry." I manage as I pull back to wipe my eyes. "I know I said I'd come here to help you with wedding preparations, to be useful, and instead I've just been..." I wave vaguely at the mess of emotions I've become, at the half-finished charcuterie board.

"Missy." Her voice is soft but fierce. "I never wanted you to come help. My only hesitation about you staying for so long was trying to figure out how to hide magic from you. Now that I don't have to do that, I'd keep you forever if I could." She brushes a strand of hair behind my ear then wipes a tear off my cheek.

My hands shake as I reach for another cookie. I'm going to make her late to her book club at the rate I'm going. "But Jules has monopolized Rachel's studio, and I've barely seen you, and I got caught up in a fling instead of helping you, and—"

"And you're allowed to have a life that isn't about making mine easier." Alex grabs my hands to still their ceaseless movement. "When are you going to understand that you don't owe me anything?"

"But you sacrificed everything for—"

"I made choices." Her fingers curl around mine, her engagement ring bumping against my knuckles. "Choices I'd make again. But they were my choices, Missy. Not chains I forged to bind you."

Something in my chest cracks. Alex must see it in my face because she does what any loving sister would do. She grabs the bottle of chocolate sprinkles, pops the lid off, and throws them at me. For a moment, I'm frozen.

The sprinkles catch in my hair, scatter across the counter, and fall between all our carefully stacked arrangements on the board. A laugh bubbles up, foreign and fragile. I grab another bottle—rainbow colored—and retaliate. Soon we're ducking and weaving around the kitchen, pelting each other with candy like we're kids again, like we're not responsible adults with careers and obligations and broken hearts.

When we finally collapse against the counter, breathless and covered in dried colored frosting, Alex touches my cheek. "When was the last time you played just because you wanted to?"

The question hits on the soft part of my heart I've been trying to hide. "I..."

"Not for an audience. Not for Jules. Not your students. Just for you?"

A memory rises unbidden—a night at the lighthouse, stars scattered across the sky outside the windows like diamonds. The moon hung low and full, painting silver across the weathered floorboard, and magic hummed in the air like a note held just beyond hearing.

Music poured through me that night—wild and wonderful, scraped raw from the deepest chambers of my heart. At some point Dean stopped playing his guitar, leaving space for me to flow into the song. It wasn't a pristine arrangement Jules had arranged or some classic, technical piece I'd practiced with Emma. No. This was something primal, something that existed in the space between magic and music, between heartbeat and harmony. Dean just happened to be there, a quiet presence that made it safe to be imperfect, to let the melody stumble and soar and break apart and reconstruct itself.

The tears start again, but different this time—not for what I've lost, but for what I'd found in those moments when I remembered how to play for the joy of it. For the way Dean's presence gave me permission to rediscover the part of myself I'd burned beneath years of perfect performances and others' expectations.

"That's what I thought," Alex says softly. She picks a sprinkle out of my hair then settles her fingers on my cheek. "So maybe the real question isn't about Dean, or Jules, or your career. Maybe it's about figuring out what you really want."

"I don't want to leave." The sob bursts from me against her shoulder. "I don't want to tour. I don't want to be perfect anymore."

Her arms tighten around me. In the background Ella croons about love and loss and finding your way home. Alex's voice is soft but sure as she strokes my hair.

"Then don't."

* * *

The recording booth at Rachel's studio feels smaller than usual, its familiar warmth replaced by a static charge of anticipation. Jules is already here, sheet music spread across multiple stands.

I clutch the unsigned contract in one hand, Giuseppe's case in the other. Both feel impossibly heavy. One holds the future I always said yes to. The other—the scratched case and everything it's come to mean—feels closer to the truth I've been trying not to name.

My pulse pounds in my ears.

Because this time, I won't smile and nod. I won't swallow my feelings or smooth over the hard edges.

This time, I'm going to say what I want.

Even if it changes everything.

"Missy!" Jules' smile is genuine, if distracted as he shuffles through the papers. "Perfect timing. I've been working on the third movement, and I think if we adjust the tempo—"

"I'm not signing the contract."

The words fall between us like a bowling ball crashing into a piano, all clanking chords and splintering wood. Jules' hands still over the sheet music, his shoulders tensing in his perfectly tailored jacket.

"I don't understand." His brow furrows. "If it's about the timing, we can be flexible. I know I showed up unexpectedly—"

"It's not that." I set the contract on a stand, careful not to disturb his organized chaos of papers. "I've been unfair to you, Jules. While I'll finish recording this album, I know I didn't contribute my share. We should renegotiate your percentage—"

"Absolutely not." He straightens until he's his usual elegant lines and practiced poise. "You inspired half of these pieces and gave suggestions that perfected the other half. The way you interpret music, how you—"

"Please." My voice catches. "Let me finish."

Something in my tone makes him pause. Maybe he hears the difference in my voice. I've been glad to go with his flow for years. But somehow I discovered a turn in the river—stumbled over him and sneezed in his face, to be specific. And maybe I didn't know my truth yet. But I was figuring it out, and I knew, at least, that it didn't follow Jules' path.

"This isn't right for me anymore." I run my fingers over Giuseppe's case, drawing strength from its familiar texture. "Even if it was my dream. It turns out what I actually want is... different."

Jules looks like I just told him he'd have to buy his next

performance suit off the rack. "What exactly are you planning to do?"

"I don't know." A laugh bubbles up, surprising me by the lightness of it. "Wait tables if I have to."

"You—Margaret Sinclair—are going to wait tables?"

I laugh. "You know I wasn't always *Margaret Sinclair*. I was once a kid with a hand-me-down cello and brown bag lunches."

"You're giving up music?" I've never seen Jules so distraught. He looks like I just told him I'd become a queen and my first decree was burning all string instruments.

"No, never. I'm going to play music that matters to me now, though."

"And what music is that?"

The question hangs in the air like a held breath. Instead of answering, I open Giuseppe's case. The familiar ritual of preparation—positioning, tightening the bow, checking the strings—steadies my hands.

"Let me show you."

I close my eyes and let myself remember—starlight through lighthouse windows, Dean's guitar weaving with my melody, magic humming in the air between the notes. The music flows through me, raw and honest and imperfect. Every measure carries the weight of recent tears in Alex's kitchen, the fierce joy of rediscovering myself, the ache of letting Dean go. I pour it all into the strings—the storm of losing him, the fear of an unmapped future, everything.

When the final note fades, I open my eyes to find Jules watching me, tears tracking silently down his cheeks. For perhaps the first time since I've known him, he seems completely lost for words. Then he breaks into applause—not his usual measured appreciation, but wild, genuine enthusiasm.

"Mon Dieu, Missy." He removes a handkerchief from his

pocket and wipes his eyes. "That was... I don't have words. You have to record your own album. This differs completely from our classical work, but—" His arms gesture wildly. "I'll pitch it myself. Handle all the details—"

"Jules." I carefully lay Giuseppe in his case. "Truly, I meant what I said. I don't want to tour anymore."

"You don't have to." He crosses to me, takes my hand in his. "But this..." He gestures to the cello. "This is real. This is music. It's what we spend our whole lives chasing." He swallows. "And you found it." A rueful laugh spills from him. "On some provincial island without a proper cup of coffee to be found anywhere."

"But there's really good pie here."

He stares at me for a moment, then bursts into a laugh. "I can concede. The pie is excellent." He gives my fingers a soft squeeze. "You've found something here, haven't you? Something beyond music."

I think of Dean's constellations, of magic shimmering in autumn air, of playing just for the joy of it. Of his dark eyes and strong arms. "Something including music," I correct gently. "But yes."

Jules releases my hands and steps back then adjusts his cuffs. "Well, then." His smile is smaller now, but free of any subterfuge. "I suppose, if you're serious..."

I nod. "I am. But I worry about your career. I didn't mean to–"

He waves my protests away. "I'll be fine, Missy. I'll have to find a new cellist. Though I doubt anyone will inspire quite the same level of compositions."

"You'll write different ones." I graze my fingers across Giuseppe's strings. "Maybe even better ones."

He chuckles. "Perhaps." Then, more seriously, he says, "But you'll think about doing a solo album? When you're ready?"

"When I'm ready."

Jules sighs, then smiles and turns toward his violin case and readies the instrument. For the first time since Jules arrived, the silence between us feels comfortable—like the rest between movements, necessary and right.

Dean

The string quartet knows their craft. Each note falls precise and pure, weaving magic through the melody in ways that make my teeth ache. I stand at the edge of Nell's wedding reception, systematically destroying a cocktail napkin while pretending to be fascinated by the table arrangements. As if I care about centerpieces when every sweep of the cello bow feels like another strike against my carefully maintained control.

Some wounds cut deeper when they heal wrong. Like scars that pulse with remembered pain, that tighten and pull when storms approach. I've spent a decade maintaining a careful distance from my family, letting guilt be my compass. Now watching Nell float through her reception in ivory lace, radiant with a joy I once stole from her, I wonder if distance was ever the answer.

The music shifts into something slower, more intimate. The kind of piece Missy would play on quiet evenings at the lighthouse, when her guard was down and her soul spilled through her fingertips. When she wasn't trying to be perfect, just real. God, even here, surrounded by family I haven't seen in years, she haunts me like an unfinished bit of magic.

Just because a melody is beautiful, doesn't mean you can capture it forever. Her words haunt me now, the way her voice had cracked on 'forever' despite the perfect performer's control. She'd twisted her hands in her sweater as she'd said it, but I don't think she noticed. God, I'd wanted to reach for her then, to brush back that strand of hair falling across her cheek, to hold her one last time. But I'd kept my hands in my pockets and maintained my distance. Head Warlock Dean Markham, always so damn in control.

Later, I'd warded my cottage until the walls hummed with contained power. Then I screamed. The magic had torn out of me like a storm, like grief given form. Books flew off shelves, windows rattled in their frames, every piece of furniture shuddered with the force of my loss. I gave in to my emotions and magic in a way I hadn't since I was a teenager. That's my role, though, isn't it? To be powerful. To be contained. To let the weight of magic and duty and position push away anyone who might get close enough to matter. To stand alone in rooms full of shattered things, pretending the broken pieces are only external.

"I was able to sneak up on the great Head Warlock, Dean Markham." Nell's voice cuts through my spiral. She stands before me in her wedding dress, eyes sparkling despite the way she nervously taps her thumb against her thigh. That's a gesture I haven't seen in so long I thought I'd forgotten it. But something within me remembers. She forces a smile. "He must have something serious on his mind."

"Forgive me." I bow formally, then immediately feel ridiculous. "Congratulations."

"Thank you." Silence stretches between us like a ward line about to break. "Are you going to spend the entire night lurking?"

"I excel at lurking. It's a professional requirement."

Her lips twitch. "Some things never change." I nod, but I'm not sure what to say. Everything has changed between us. We'd once been inseparable. Now I don't even know how to speak to her. She shrugs like she's trying to pull on a jacket that no longer fits. "Could I convince you to dance with me?"

The question catches me off guard. For a moment I'm frozen, caught between old guilt and new hope. But her hand is already extended, and some choices make themselves. "Of course."

We sweep onto the dance floor, and it hits me how grown she looks. She's pulled her dark waves back into a sleek chignon at the nape of her neck, and her jewelry exudes sophistication rather than the playfulness of the pieces she wore the last time I saw her. My little sister, the one I used to chase around with sparklers, now stands my height in heels. The string quartet plays something achingly beautiful, and I'm drowning in memories of another musician, another dance, another person I let slip through my fingers.

"Head Warlock of Magnolia Cove by thirty." Nell's voice carries that familiar teasing lilt. "Always the overachiever."

"Leading researcher at Calthorne. Always the perfectionist. Plus I noticed half of who's who in Willow Bay is here." The words come easier than expected. "Always the popular one as well."

She smiles, soft and real. "You attended."

"Yes."

"I wasn't sure you received my invitation."

I stop dancing. "Your invitation? I thought Mom sent it. I assumed you wouldn't want me here."

Dancers in evening dress whirl around us and the music swells. But Nell's attention remains on me, her brow furrowing. "Mom thought adding a note from her might help. I thought you wouldn't want to come."

"I didn't." She winces and I scramble to find my voice before bungling things between us again. "I mean, because my presence would remind you of how I hurt you." The words scrape my throat. "You told me that you never wanted to see me again."

She looks away but I see the shimmer in her eyes before she does. "Dean, I was seventeen. That was a decade ago. I know I said terrible things to you, but I was young and stupid and hurt. I needed time to heal. And you were barely more than a kid, and you were doing your best." She touches my arm, and the contact burns like truth. "When you wiped everyone's memories..."

I shudder, mint-sharp regret flooding my mouth.

"...you were protecting everyone, and I was too young and hurt and foolish to understand that."

"I destroyed your happiness."

"I thought I'd destroyed yours." A gasp spills out of me and I look at my sister, at the makeup smearing beneath her eyes. She swallows. "Once I realized how selfish I'd been and processed the hurt, you were already established in Magnolia Cove. I didn't know what to say, and I didn't want to destroy your chance at happiness." Her face loses color as she speaks and her voice is whisper-soft so I strain to hear her over the music. "So I decided to say nothing. I thought coming back here would just remind you of all the time you'd lost because of my selfishness, so I kept my distance."

Ten years. I've spent ten years building my life around her absence, letting guilt shape every decision, every achievement. Head Warlock of Magnolia Cove before thirty—not because I craved power, but because I needed purpose heavy enough to anchor me against the weight of what I'd done. Or what I thought I'd done.

The sharp taste of memory magic floods my mouth again,

but this time it carries a different bitterness. Mom is right. Nell and I are both too damn stubborn.

I've crafted every bit of magic, reinforced every ward, maintained every barrier with the precision of someone who believes isolation is their penance. Built my reputation on control and distance because I thought that's what she needed —her brother, the one who destroyed her happiness, far enough away that she could heal. And all this time, she's carried the same guilt, thinking she'd driven me away.

She glances around the reception, at her new husband dancing with Mom, but also throwing her concerned looks. "Mom convinced me to invite you. But I didn't want to guilt you and force you to attend, so I just sent the invitation."

"Nell." I gasp, unable to find words that can match my racing thoughts. "I ruined your life."

"No, I ruined my life." Her cheeks flush but she raises her chin. "And it taught me some painful but valuable lessons. Sometimes the rules exist for good reason. But sometimes... you just know... sometimes love is worth the risk." She swallows and bats more tears away and that's when I realize I'm crying too. She grabs my hand, tentatively and I accept the gesture. "And I'm so glad you took the risk and came home."

The words hit like an echo of Missy's goodbye. Of another choice made from love, another sacrifice offered to protect someone else's happiness. I've been so focused on maintaining distance that I missed how bridges can be rebuilt, how some wounds need connection to heal properly.

Maybe it's time to stop letting old scars dictate new choices.

"Have breakfast with me tomorrow?" Nell's question comes hesitantly, but her eyes are wide with hope. She wants to spend time with me. Wants to see me again.

"What about your new husband?"

"We have a three-week honeymoon in the Seychelles." She

grins, looking so much like the little sister I remember my chest aches. "I've had him for four years. I want a few hours with my brother. If he would want that with me."

"Of course I would, Nell."

The next moment shatters a decade of careful distance. We collide in a tangle of wedding dress and dark suit, tears and laughter mixing like conflicting spells. My magic sparks against her skin, recognizing family bonds that run deeper than duty or guilt.

She smells like gardenias and salty tears, and her grip is fierce enough to wrinkle my jacket beyond salvation. It's one of the happiest moments I've had in years.

* * *

Morning finds us at an old favorite cafe, sunlight spilling across a table laden with pastries neither of us has touched. Nell stirs her tea gracefully, and I catalog the changes in her—the confident set of her shoulders, the ease in her smile, the way she holds herself like someone who knows who she is. This is a version of my sister I don't know.

The minty tang of old magic ghosts my tongue as she speaks. But watching her talk about her research, her new life, her plans, I see the scars of old wounds—still visible, but no longer raw. She's mostly healed, the way broken bones knit stronger at the fracture points. But there's still something tentative in how she leans forward, in the way her fingers trace the rim of her teacup when she mentions our parents. Like she's built a beautiful life but left space in it, waiting for the last pieces to slot into place. Waiting, maybe, for me.

"Dean?" Her voice shifts, knowing. "What's really on your mind?"

"I've been such a fool about this. I thought I was being strong for you. I thought your silence meant you needed me gone, and I convinced myself that protecting you meant staying away."

I roll a sugar packet between my fingers, needing something to ground me against the tide of emotion threatening to crack my careful control.

Nell's fingers clench around her teacup, her knuckles whitening against the delicate china. "And I was too proud to reach out first. Too afraid you'd reject me after everything I said. I told myself you were happy in Magnolia Cove, that you'd built this perfect life without us. That reaching out would disrupt your carefully constructed world." A bitter laugh escapes her. "I even convinced myself it was selfless letting you have your space, your success. When really, I was just protecting myself from having to face what I'd done."

Her dark eyes glimmer, but if she feels like crying, she fights back the urge. A skill I've also mastered.

"We're quite the pair, aren't we?" I offer, my voice rough. "Both so determined to protect each other that we forgot how to be siblings."

"Stubbornness is a Markham family trait." We both laugh and she continues on tentatively. "You know, if you wanted to come home... I mean, you probably have people you care about in Magnolia Cove. Or maybe someone special?"

I look away, but Nell's question hangs in the air like magic, impossible to ignore. The cafe's morning bustle fades to background noise as memories of Missy surface—her music weaving through my magic, her laugh breaking through my defense, her goodbye etched into my heart like a knife carving into a tree, cutting down to the sap.

"There was someone." The words taste like regret and there's no flavor that matches that. "She's..." How do I explain her? The way she made colors brighter just by existing in my world. How she saw through every barrier I'd built without even trying? "She's a musician. A cellist. But she ended things because she thought she was protecting me. Protecting my relationship with our parents."

I rip open the sugar packet and pour the contents into my tea. Each word feels scraped from somewhere too raw to touch. "She encouraged me to attend the wedding. Said I shouldn't lose my family over her."

"This is Missy?"

I lifted my spoon to stir the tea but set it back down and stare at my sister.

Color stains her cheek but she shrugs. "Mom told me about her."

"Yes," I all but spit the word. "Missy."

My tea sits untouched, sugar crystals settling to the bottom like sediment, like all the things I can't quite say. Mom would have told Nell everything, then—how they caught us at the festival, how Missy's mere presence threatened their precious rules. The way they'd looked at her like she was a curse made flesh, a danger to be contained rather than a woman who made music feel like pure enchantment.

"Mom and Dad would never accept her." My gaze has gone distant to a window smudged with children's fingerprints. "She knew it. She saw their faces, felt their judgement. Something about her always affected my magic, intensifying it. It's like I could feel the pain she experienced that night. So she did what she thought was right. Encouraged me to choose my family. And I did what I thought was right. To let her go so I don't cause her more of that pain."

My fingers curl around the teacup, and I take a long swallow of the too-bitter brew—most of the sugar still clumped uselessly at the bottom. "The thing is, Missy wasn't wrong. I couldn't fight her decision because I couldn't promise her happiness. I couldn't let her sacrifice her joy to be with someone when our parents would never accept her."

Nell's frown has deepened until it's pressed thick lines on

either side of her mouth. "Are you sure you couldn't make it work?"

I jerk my gaze up to meet hers. How could she ask that? She's already heard Mom's side. She already knows Missy is right. Our parents would be a thorn in our side if we were together, or a silent absence that Missy would inevitably blame herself for. And I won't set her up for misery. "How could it? Her sister's involved in our world, yes, but she's still non-magical. I'm Head Warlock, a Markham, I have duties and—"

"Wait." Nell sets down her cup with a sharp clink. "Her sister knows about magic?"

"Alex. Yes, she's marrying a local."

"And you said Missy affects your magic somehow?"

I guess I had said that. "The wards... they strengthen when she plays. Her music makes everything more intense but somehow easier to control. But she's—"

"A Resonant." Nell practically vibrates with excitement. "She must be."

"A what?"

"We've been researching them at Calthorne." Words tumble out of her as she leans forward. "The information is new, very experimental, but more and more we're discovering that some humans have a natural harmonic with magical energy. They can't perform magic themselves but they amplify it, strengthen it. It's incredibly rare, but..." Her eyes sparkle. "It often runs in families."

"Alex." Understanding strikes like lightning. "That's why she saw through the wards so easily."

"Exactly!" Nell has come alive. Her hands whip around as she talks. "And you say Missy's a musician? Resonants are almost always artists. Their creativity naturally attunes them to magical frequencies."

"But the council's rule about humans—"

"Were made before we understood Resonants." She waves

away my protest. "Dean, think about it. She strengthens your magic. She naturally perceives magical energy. Her sister's already part of our world. The universe practically gift-wrapped her for you."

I take a swallow of the tea and grimace when I realize once again that I'd still forgotten to mix in the sugar. "It doesn't matter now. She's leaving on tour."

"Says who?"

"She has a contract..."

"Because you gave her no reason to stay!" Nell pounds the table with her fist, rattling the china. "God, you really are as stubborn and bullheaded as I am."

"Mom and Dad would never—"

"Let me work on Mom and Dad." Nell's smile turns wicked. "Go get her. Before she leaves thinking she has to sacrifice her happiness for yours."

The server drops by with fresh cups of tea and takes away the one I barely touched. My parents' disapproval weighs heavier than a boulder, but something nags at my thoughts. I've bent rules for Alex and Missy, made exceptions I'd never consider for other humans. Because somehow, deep in my bones where magic lives, I knew they were different. This Resonant business—it explains everything.

The way the wards sing when Missy plays, how her music weaves through magical currents like it belongs there, how Alex sensed magic from the beginning.

I can hear Grammie Rae's voice in my mind. *The magic knows who it wants.* At least she isn't here for this conversation. She'd probably elbow me again and cackle loudly enough to draw half the cafe's attention.

"No." The word comes out stronger than I expected, carrying the weight of decision. It's Head Warlock Dean Markham's voice as I've never heard it before. "I'm going to convince Mom and Dad myself. You're right, Nell. I should have fought. Should have the hard conversations instead of letting my pride convince me that pushing everyone away was noble."

Nell's grin turns as fierce as flames. "Hell yes! That's the brother I remember." She tucks a strand of dark hair behind her ear, her smile softening as she looks at me. "Oh, and when I'm in the Seychelles, I'll actually send you a postcard this time —so you'll know it's from me."

"I'd rather visit." The words make her eyebrows jump up. "Once you're back. If that's okay."

"Of course it's okay." Her eyes are shimmering again but then they glisten with mischief instead. "And I hope to get to meet this Missy of yours then too."

Hope blooms in my chest like learning how to manage magic. "I hope so too."

Some patterns demand to be broken. Some songs refuse to end until every note finds its rightful place. And something deep in my bones knows mine and Missy's song isn't over yet.

Missy

The Hungry Gull's neon signs hum softly, casting their glow into the darkening world. Laughter and conversation fill the air as Hazel weaves through the red vinyl booths, passing out slices of cherry pie so good people are licking their plates clean, and coffee cups that remain mostly untouched. Ethan grimaces as Hazel sets a mug before him, but I take a long sip from mine—sometimes I like to remind myself of the taste of terrible midnight airport coffee.

I'm wedged into a booth across from Alex, watching Tom attempt to build a tower out of coffee creamers while Rachel shares stories about band class that morning.

"And then," Rachel wheezes through laughter, her coffee untouched and cooling aside Tom's increasingly precarious creamer tower, "Mikey decided his saxophone needed more *pizzazz* and tried his hand at unauthorized magic. The next thing I know, cherry blossoms are shooting out of every instrument in the room!" Her eyes widen. "Especially the tubas!"

"Oh my god," Zoe throws her head back and roars with laughter. "I always admire a good rebellion. Band kids for life, am I right?"

"Heck yeah!" Tom reaches across the table to high-five her with such enthusiasm that his creamer tower collapses. The tiny containers scatter across the red vinyl like dominos, and he lets out a groan that would do any defeated architect proud.

Rachel continues without even acknowledging the disaster. "And then poor Emma starts sneezing like she's providing percussion for the entire orchestra. Turns out she's allergic to cherry blossoms."

"That kid is going to be in so much trouble," Ethan says, but his eyes are soft with amusement.

Rachel's grin turns conspiratorial as she leans forward. "Nah, I didn't write him up." She winks at Zoe. "Band kids for life, right? We stick together."

Something warm unfurls in my chest at their easy camaraderie, at the way their shared history weaves through their words like a familiar refrain. This is what I've been missing on tour—not just a place to belong, but people who understand that belonging isn't about being perfect. It's about being real, about making mistakes and having others catch you when you fall.

A shadow passes over the warmth of the moment, like a cloud moving in front of the sun. Two issues still loom before me. The first is practical but daunting—I have a decent nest egg from touring, enough to buy a small place here and get settled, but money has a way of getting spent. Without a steady income, my future looks less than secure.

But the second issue... my fingers find the rim of my coffee cup and trace its circumference. Dean. Living in the town he essentially conducts while trying to avoid him is going to be like attempting to play a duet with someone you can't look at. Impossible and painful and probably destined for disaster.

"We're out of sugar." Violet levels this at Tom as though his creamer stack is to blame for the critical shortage in sweetener.

Tom responds by sticking out his tongue. Violet mirrors the gesture immediately. Laughter ripples through the group and I smile.

"I'll grab some," I say as I slide out of the booth.

Rachel joins me. "Actually, I've wanted to talk with you one-on-one if I could grab you for a minute."

"Sure, of course." We make it to the condiment station tucked against the far wall stacked with ketchup, maple syrup, and the desired sugar packets.

Rachel leans against the wall. "Alex was discussing you moving here, and I had an idea. Grant and I are stretched thin between my teaching and leading the music program and his *ice cream empire*..." She chuckles. "We could really use someone to run the summer music camp for us."

I straighten, something like hope thrumming beneath my ribs. "I'm all ears. And desperately in want of a job that doesn't involve playing wedding marches for tourists at the bed-and-breakfast."

Rachel grins. "I thought you'd be the perfect fit. Someone passionate, someone who really understands both the technical side and the heart of music. Someone who can nurture young talent while keeping the magic of music alive."

The more she speaks the faster my heart beats and I'm clutching sugar packets so tight I'm going to crush them, spilling crystals over the peeling linoleum.

This job is perfect for me. Winter would be mine for composition, those long quiet months when the island wraps itself in stillness and possibility. I could pour my soul into creating without the pressure of performance deadlines or critics' expectations. Spring would bloom with preparation, and summer... summer would be for sharing music's magic with young minds, watching talent unfold.

"Oh my god, that would be amazing."

"Really?" Rachel grabs my hands and now we're both crushing the sugar.

"Yes, I'd really, really love to."

"That's so great! I can't wait to tell Grant." She snorts. "He's hoping we might actually get a vacation in one of these days."

I open my mouth but before I can respond, the first notes of a guitar cut through the diner's chatter. The sound is achingly familiar—not a precise classical arrangement, but something rawer, more honest.

My heart recognizes the melody before my mind catches up. "Beyond the Sea." I turn slowly, already knowing from the sound who I'm going to find but needing to see him, anyway.

Dean stands just inside the doorway, his black leather jacket a stark contrast to the diner's cheerful colors. His fingers move over guitar strings with careful grace, and when he sings, his voice echoes through the quiet. Quiet because the entire diner has fallen silent, watching their stern, distant Head Warlock transform—like a caterpillar emerging as a butterfly, something almost unrecognizable and utterly impossible to ignore.

Zoe's mouth hangs open, Tom's coffee cup is frozen halfway to his lips, and even Alex's eyes are wide. Hazel, who's seen five decades of drama unfold in this diner, has stopped wiping down the counter to stare. This is Dean as they've never seen him—vulnerable, his carefully maintained facade falling away note by note.

His eyes find mine across the distance, and the world narrows to this moment—this impossible, beautiful collision of everything I thought I had to choose between. Magic and music. Duty and desire. Perfect and real.

When he reaches me, the last notes hang in the utter silence of the diner. "Dean?"

"Missy." He swallows hard, glancing around at our frozen

audience before focusing entirely on me. Gone is the careful control, the stern facade. This is Dean stripped to his essence, as vulnerable as a song played in darkness echoing off lighthouse walls. "I've been prideful and foolish. I wanted to protect you from everything—judgment, my own fears, and the complications of being with someone like me. But I'm tired of letting fear orchestrate my life. I'm in love with you, Missy Sinclair."

A gasp escapes me, the sound almost lost in the profound silence of the diner. Someone—probably Grammie Rae—whispers, "Finally!" followed by several sharp shushes.

"What about your family?" The question comes out barely above a whisper.

"I spoke with them. They understand—enough at least." A smile tugs at his mouth. "I've thought a lot about what you said, and I've decided I like records, even if the melody doesn't perfectly capture the moment. Some songs do last forever. And this?" He gestures between us. "It's the most important melody I've ever known."

My heart thunders, keeping time with hope and possibility. Dean continues, words tumbling out faster now. "I know you're leaving for the tour, but we can make it work if you want that. I can wait, I can—"

"I'm not." I take a step closer to him. We're like actors on a stage, but for the first time in my life, I'm not performing. The familiar weight of an audience's attention rests on my shoulders, but this moment strips away every practiced smile, every polished gesture I've spent years perfecting. This is just me and Dean, creating something raw and real in the space between heartbeats. It's the most honest thing I've ever done, because it isn't a performance at all—it's simple truth, set to the melody of my racing heart. "I'm not going on tour. I didn't sign the contract."

"You're not leaving?" His voice breaks on the last word.

"I'm staying here." I step closer still, close enough to see the flecks of amber in his dark eyes. "Actually, I just agreed to run the summer music camp. I was plotting how to avoid running into you and making things awkward." A small laugh escapes me, genuine and breathless. "But Magnolia Cove is a pretty small town. It might be easier if I didn't need to do that after all."

He grins, and judging by the raised eyebrows around us, I'm pretty sure people are just as stunned by that as they were by him singing and playing the guitar. But my attention snaps back to him as he speaks, his voice light as a feather. "You're staying here?"

I smile, my voice soft but sure. "I'm staying. For good. For me." My fingers find the edge of his leather jacket, anchoring myself to this moment. "And maybe, if you want, for us."

Dean's free hand comes up to cup my cheek, his touch reverent as though he's handling something precious and rare. The calluses on his fingertips from years of secret guitar playing graze my skin, and the sensation sends a shiver through me. "I want that more than anything."

Around us, the diner holds its collective breath. The neon signs cast their gentle glow, painting Dean's dark eyes with hints of electric blue, and in them I see every possibility I'd been afraid to hope for. This is what Alex sees when she looks at Ethan, I realize. Not perfection, but something better— something real.

"Well?" Grammie Rae's voice cuts through the silence. "Are you two going to kiss already or do we have to wait another six months?"

Laughter ripples through the crowd, breaking the spell of silence. Dean's ears turn pink, but his smile doesn't falter. If anything, it grows wider, more certain. His guitar shifts to his back as he pulls me closer.

"What do you say?" he breathes against my lips.

"Yes."

I've said yes hundreds of times in my life. Yes to Juilliard, where perfect technique was practically a requirement for entry. Yes to endless tours that left my soul as empty as the concert halls after the crowds departed. Yes to Jules and our album, to encore performances that felt like echoes of something I'd lost along the way. Each yes had been a step farther from myself, a note played precisely but without heart.

But this yes resonates through me like the first time I truly heard music—not just with my ears but with my whole being. It's yes to morning light streaming through lighthouse windows, to magic dancing in the air when we play together. Yes to a small town where imperfect notes create the most beautiful melodies. Yes to Dean Markham, who guards his heart as carefully as he guards his town, yet stands before me offering both without reservation.

This yes feels like coming home to a song I've always known but never quite managed to play. Until now.

When our lips meet, it's nothing like our desperate kisses in the lighthouse or our careful stolen ones at the studio. This kiss tastes like possibility, like the first notes of a composition we'll spend years together writing. His arms wrap around me, solid and sure, and then he dips me low, kissing me like he means it, like the world has fallen away. The diner erupts in cheers and applause and what sounds suspiciously like Tom whistling through his fingers.

When I'm back fully on my feet, I drink in the sight of Dean Markham—stern Head Warlock, secret musician, and now, impossibly, mine—looking at me like I'm everything he's ever wanted.

The cheers last so long that heat creeps up my neck and even Dean's cheeks are flushed. But there's something magical about it too—about letting the whole town witness the crumbling of the careful walls we've built.

Dean's fingers find mine and he speaks to me like we're entirely alone, not standing before a crowded diner. "I spent so long thinking I had to choose between duty and desire."

I chuckle. "Me too. Has your stance changed any now?"

He brushes hair back that doesn't need to be fixed and smiles. "Now I understand some things are meant to harmonize."

Around us, the diner slowly returns to its familiar rhythm. Hazel resumes her coffee rounds, the gentle clink of cups keeping time with quiet conversations. Tom rebuilds his creamer tower, Zoe and Rachel fall into some passionate debate, and Alex just winks at me before taking her seat.

And here, in the heart of it all, Dean and I are creating our own symphony—one made of lighthouse secrets and unspoken magic, of broken rules and mended hearts.

Some songs, after all, last forever. And ours is just beginning.

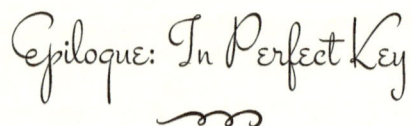

Epilogue: In Perfect Key

Missy

The cobblestones of Main Street look almost dreamlike in twilight's watercolor hues tonight. Dean's hand is warm in mine as we walk. Magic shimmers in the air, easy to see now that I know what to look for. It's like starlight caught in amber, like music made tangible.

Dean explained about Resonants—humans with natural magical attunement—his eyes lighting up as he spoke. He's been adorably enthusiastic about researching it, requesting studies from other communities. I let him explain the theories, but honestly? I don't need scientific explanations or magical theorems to understand what I know in my soul. I'm supposed to be here. I knew it before and this theory only confirms it.

"Hi Missy! Hi Dean!" Iris waves as she passes, her arms full of late-blooming chrysanthemums that seem to dance with each step she takes.

Dean startles slightly at the casual greeting, and I can't help but laugh though I do my best to muffle it. He's still adjusting to this—to being seen as more than just the stern Head Warlock, to belonging rather than standing apart. The transformation reminds me of watching a tightly wound string slowly release its tension and finding its natural resonance.

"You'll get used to it," I whisper and squeeze his hand.

His smile comes easier these days, and he almost sounds not-cranky when he says, "I suppose I will."

And he will. Just like I'm getting used to this new life I've chosen—running the summer music program, composing without pressure, loving freely. Even our upcoming visit to his family feels more like anticipation than anxiety. The melodies that once felt trapped beneath technical perfection now flow freely, filling my mind with possibilities. I haven't told Jules yet, but I've decided to record an album. And I'm just corny enough to title it *Cello Magic*.

A chill whispers through the ocean's breeze, carrying winter's first promise. Dean pulls me closer as we approach the Whimsical Whisk, its window glowing with warmth despite the *Closed* sign. Inside, familiar voices and laughter spill out like music.

The bell chimes as we enter, and I'm immediately wrapped in Alex's embrace. Dean is absorbed into the fray by Ethan who's been making a real effort to include him. The whole book club has gathered for wedding cake tasting. Tom and Violet argue playfully over flavor combinations, Rachel and Grant listen stoically as Zoe presents each option with theatrical flair, and Mia smirks at her wife and shakes her head. Rhianna and Eli, who I've yet to meet, have returned from their latest adventure, their faces sun-kissed and happy.

"So this is the woman who melted our resident grumpy warlock." The woman who has to be Rhianna with her curls knotted back with a pencil and a pin on her cardigan that says 'shelf care is self-care' grins at me as she extends her hand.

"Rhianna, by the way. I have to say I'm impressed. We were taking bets on whether he even knew how to smile."

"Told you he was dateable," Alex says with a smirk.

"Isn't it cheating if you talked your sister into it?" Rhianna crosses her arms and turns on my sister.

Alex rolls her eyes, but her smile is fond. "As if anyone could talk Missy into anything."

The truth of those words settles into my chest. There was a time when that wasn't true—when I'd shaped myself to others' expectations like a melody conforming to someone else's arrangement. But now I know my own voice, understand my own rhythms.

Dean approaches then, his posture still carrying that careful control, though it softens when he meets my eyes. "Rhianna."

"Hey... Dean." She laughs awkwardly. "Nice weather we're having, huh?"

His nod is pure Head Warlock, but when I nudge him, his expression warms. "It's been a mild autumn. That's always nice."

Rhianna stares at him like a gargoyle just spoke and I'm once again biting back a laugh. Progress, one note at a time.

Zoe's voice cuts through the chatter as she presents her latest creation. "Behold! Lavender-honey buttercream with elderflower sponge and edible gold leaf." The cake sparkles with barely contained magic. "Tell me this isn't the most exciting wedding cake concept you've ever seen."

"It's beautiful, Zoe," Alex says.

Zoe props a hand on a hip. "You don't like it, though, do you?" She stabs a knife into it. "Don't tell me you're going to be one of those tragic vanilla-and-buttercream couples. Next you'll tell me you want the most basic roses piped on the cake. My artistic soul can't take this level of betrayal."

Mia passes around samples and we all start nibbling them,

the flavors exploding in my mouth—each bite revealing new depths and complexities. And the feeling—the magic—tastes exactly how happily ever after would taste. I catch Dean's eye and my heart swells with recognition. Because I already know this flavor, this blend of sweetness and certainty.

Alex finishes her bite. "It's delicious, Zoe."

Zoe props both fists on her hips. "But?"

"I do really like vanilla cake." Alex almost winces when she says it.

Ethan wraps an arm around her waist. "Whatever Alex likes is perfect to me."

"You two are literally a tragedy." Zoe throws her hands up. "I'm trying to create art here!"

"Well…" Alex exchanges a look with Ethan, one of those silent conversations they've mastered. "We've actually been thinking. One cake seems… limiting, especially given the talent we have at our disposal." Her eyes sparkle as they meet Ethan's again before returning to Zoe. "What if we gave you creative license over an entire cake table? Something that really lets you showcase your artistic vision?"

Zoe freezes mid-gesture, her eyes widening like Alex just told her they discovered a new flavor of sugar. "An entire table?" A grin breaks across her face and her eyes have gone bright and wild. "Now you're speaking my language, Sugar. I only have a few months left, though. I need to plan."

I chuckle as Dean and I drift to a quiet corner with other samples Mia has produced. His fingers trace patterns on my hand as we taste each option and Tom expounds on the possibilities now that they have an *in* with the Head Warlock. "Just think of the magical potential," he says, gesturing at Dean without looking at him and therefore missing the skeptical lift of his brow. "We could really push the boundaries of enchanted pastries."

"My desserts stand on their own." Zoe crosses her arms

and her tattoos peek past her sweater's sleeves. "They don't need magical flair."

Tom scoffs. "You literally love flair."

Rhianna giggles from across the room. "Who doesn't?"

Their voices and laughter fade into a pleasant hum as I turn my attention back to Dean. He's watching me with that softness that still makes my heart skip—the way his careful control melts at the edges when we're together, like frost yielding to spring sunshine.

He gestures with his fork at his empty plate. "They're all excellent. Do you think you'd have the Whisk make your wedding cake one day?"

I go still, my fork suspended halfway to my mouth. Dean blinks, his mouth falling open slightly, as if to backpedal, but no words come out. His hand drops the fork with a clatter, and he quickly picks it up, gripping it too tightly. A flush creeps up his neck to his ears, and he shifts in his chair, suddenly hyper-focused on the smudge of frosting on the edge of his plate. "I mean... if that's something you'd ever... you know... want. Not that you—uh." His voice fades, and he stabs at an invisible crumb, his gaze fixed anywhere but on me.

I laugh first. Then Dean joins me and the tension dissolves into something sweeter than any of Zoe's creations.

"Of course," I say, squeezing his hand. "What's a brother-in-law for if he doesn't make my cake?" Our eyes meet, and in that look I see our future stretching out before us like an unfinished song waiting to be written. "Besides, you know I'm going to have to play at their wedding. I'd say they owe me."

"That sounds fair."

Around us, the Whisk hums with magic and laughter, with friendship and possibility. Dean's thumb brushes across my knuckles, and I lean into him, savoring this moment of perfect imperfection. This is what I was searching for all those years on stage—not the perfect performance, but genuine connection. Not technical precision, but real magic.

Some songs take time to find their true melody. Beethoven spent a decade refining his Ninth Symphony, searching for something that speaks to the soul. Two centuries later, it's a masterpiece that echoes in every grand music hall around the world. I meet Dean's dark eyes, his soft smile, that rare thing he offers only to me. And it strikes me—that's the magic of a truly great song. Once it finds its harmony, it doesn't just resonate, it lingers, timeless and unforgettable.

Next Book

Loved *Strings Attached*? More love is in the air in Magnolia Cove...

Alex and Ethan are finally getting married—and Magnolia Cove is pulling out all the stops.

If you love swoony banter, small-town magic, and fake dating that feels a little *too* real, you won't want to miss *To Have and To Pretend*—a friends-to-lovers romance filled with wit, warmth, and just the right amount of magical chaos.

This time, the spotlight's on Iris Morrowind—florist, secret romantic, and champion bouquet enchantress—and Tom Bryson, her steady, salt-sweet best friend who's been by her side since childhood. A bachelorette party, a family match-making scheme, and one impulsive pact to play each other's plus-one set them on a path where pretending stops feeling so pretend.

Fake dating pact? Check.

Friends-to-lovers slow burn? Absolutely.

Moonlit flowers, meddling families, and a guaranteed happily-ever-after? Always.

So grab your favorite bouquet, settle in somewhere cozy,

and return to Magnolia Cove for a love story that will leave you smiling, sighing, and maybe believing that sometimes the best romances start with a little pretending.

Pick Up *To Have and To Pretend* and prepare to fall in love all over again...

Dean's Favorite Autumn Spice Cookies

Dean's mother always baked a batch or three of these cookies when the leaves began to turn. Now, years later, Dean still swears he can taste that same love in every cinnamon-laced bite. When Missy pulls a tin of them from one of his mother's care packages, the scent alone—warm spice, sugar, and memory—has a way of softening even the sternest warlock edges. Sweet, simple, and just a little bit magical.

Ingredients:

- 2 ¼ cups (280g) all-purpose flour
- ½ teaspoon baking soda
- ½ teaspoon salt
- 1 ½ teaspoons ground cinnamon
- ½ teaspoon ground ginger
- ¼ teaspoon ground nutmeg
- ¾ cup (170g) unsalted butter, softened
- 1 cup (200g) packed brown sugar
- 1 large egg
- 1 teaspoon vanilla extract

Instructions:

1. Preheat oven to 350°F (175°C). Line two baking sheets with parchment paper.
2. In a medium bowl, whisk together flour, baking soda, salt, and spices.
3. In a large bowl, cream butter and brown sugar until light and fluffy. Beat in egg and vanilla.
4. Add dry ingredients gradually, mixing just until combined.
5. Scoop dough into tablespoon-sized balls and place on baking sheets, leaving space to spread.
6. Bake for 10–12 minutes, until edges are golden brown and centers are set.
7. Cool on the sheet for a few minutes before moving to a wire rack. Best enjoyed warm, with someone you love enough to share the last cookie.

Tips to Fall In Love*:

- Cinnamon should be bold, not shy. Don't skimp.
- Magic isn't always about spells—sometimes it's just the right mix of sugar and spice.
- When in doubt, slice the last cookie in half. It tastes better when shared.

*Sorry for the pun; I had to.

Acknowledgments

Every book is its own kind of symphony, and this one wouldn't exist without some very special people lending their notes along the way.

Milly—your guidance and encouragement have been the steady rhythm behind my writing journey. Thank you for reminding me how to lean into romance, for celebrating the highs, and for giving me the tools to navigate the tricky passages. This story sings brighter because of you.

To my husband—you make the house smell like fresh coffee every morning (which I don't even drink, but love the smell), and you never fail to encourage my collection of softest sweaters and coziest blankets. You are are like autumn—all my favorite things bundled together.

To Jamie, my brilliant beta reader—your insights and thoughtful feedback helped bring this book into harmony. Thank you for shining light on the places that needed it most and helping me find the truest melody in Missy's journey.

To Megan, master of proofreading who even caught title inconsistencies in this series (Easter egg if you want to go looking!)—you always catch the smallest details and help these books shine.

To Monique, my son's wonderful cello teacher—thank you for patiently answering my questions and sharing your expertise, which gave Missy's musical world the authenticity it needed. I'm so grateful for your generosity.

To my daughter—I know, I know, I wrote my first musician heroine as a cellist instead of a pianist. Seven years of your practice deserved better. Consider this my official apology (and maybe a promise that I'll try to make the next musician I write a pianist!)

To my friends and family—thank you for loving me through the chaos of deadlines and drafts, and for reminding me, always, that I'm never truly doing this alone.

And to you, dear readers—thank you for returning to Magnolia Cove, for believing in magic woven through everyday life, and for trusting me to bring you another love story. Your support means more than words can capture.

With deepest gratitude and love,

-Noel